Mrs. Henry Wood

Court Netherleigh

A Novel. Vol. 2. Second Edition

Mrs. Henry Wood

Court Netherleigh
A Novel. Vol. 2. Second Edition

ISBN/EAN: 9783337047344

Printed in Europe, USA, Canada, Australia, Japan

Cover: Foto ©Andreas Hilbeck / pixelio.de

More available books at **www.hansebooks.com**

A Novel.

BY

MRS. HENRY WOOD,

AUTHOR OF " EAST LYNNE," "THE CHANNINGS,"
ETC. ETC.

IN THREE VOLUMES.
VOL. II.

SECOND EDITION.

LONDON:

RICHARD BENTLEY & SON, NEW BURLINGTON STREET,
Publishers in Ordinary to Her Majesty.
1881.

LONDON:

PRINTED BY J. OGDEN AND CO.,

172, ST, JOHN STREET, E.C.

CONTENTS.

———◆◆◆———

CHAPTER I.

THE DAY OF RECKONING.

THE continuous hum of the busy London world came floating drowsily in through a bed-room window in Berkeley Street, open to the hot and brilliant summer day, and falling, unnoticed, upon the ears of Mrs. Oscar Dalrymple.

"What an idiot I have been!" soliloquised she. "And what a cat that Damereau is!"

The above pretty speech—not at all suitable for pretty lips—was given vent to by Selina on her return from that morning visit to her milliner, when the latter had wholly refused to listen to reason, and both had lost their courtesy.

Her dainty bonnet tossed on the bed, her little black lace mantle on the back of her low dressing-chair, Selina, who had come straight home, swayed herself backwards and forwards in the said chair, as she mentally ran over the items of the keen words just exchanged between herself and madame, and wondered what in the world she was to do.

"If I had but kept my temper!" she thought, in self-reproach. "It was always a fault of mine to be quick and fiery—like poor Robert. It was nothing but that which made her so angry. What on earth would become of me if she should do as she says—send the account to Oscar?"

Selina started up at the thought. Calmly equable to a rather remarkable degree in general, she was one of the most restless of human beings when she did give way to excitement. Just as Robert had been.

"If he had but lived!" she cried, tears filling her eyes as her thoughts reverted to her brother, "I'd have taken this trouble to him and he would have settled it. Robert was so generous!"

But Selina quite forgot to recall the fact that her brother's income, at the best, would not have been larger than her husband's was. Not quite as large, indeed, for Oscar had his own small patrimony of six or seven hundred a year in addition. Just now she could not be expected to remember common sense.

The Dalrymples had a distant cousin, a merchant, or cotton broker, or something of the kind, residing in Liverpool, who was supposed to be fabulously rich. He had quarrelled with the family long ago, and was looked upon as no better than an ill-natured, growling bear. An idea had come into Selina's brain lately — what if she wrote to tell him her position and beg a little money from his rich coffers to set her straight? It came to her again now, as she sat there. But no! That ungenial man was known to hold unseemly debt and extravagance of all kinds in especial abhorrence. He would only write her a condemnatory answer; perhaps even re-enclose her begging letter to Oscar! Selina started from the thought, and put away for ever all notion of aid from Benjamin Dalrymple.

"How is this woman to be pacified?" she resumed, her reflections reverting to Madame Damereau. "What a simpleton I was to provoke her! Two or three hundred pounds might do it for the present. Where am I to get them? If she carries out this dreadful threat and appeals to Oscar, what should I do? What *could* I do? And all the world would know—Oh!" she shivered, "I must stop that. *I* must get some from him, if I can. I will try at once. Ugh; what a calamity the want of money is!"

She descended the stairs and entered the dining-room, where her husband was. He sat at the table, writing letters, and seemed to be in the midst of business accounts.

"Oscar!"

He looked up. "What is it?"

"Oscar," she said, advancing to stand close to him, "can you, please, let me have a little money?"

"No, that I can't, Selina. I am settling up a few payments now, and can only do it by halves. Others I am writing to put off entirely for the present."

He had bent over his writing again, as if the question, being answered, was done with.

"Oscar, I must have it."

"What money do you mean? Some for housekeeping? I can let you have that."

"No, no: for myself. I want—I want—two hundred pounds," she said, jerking it out. She did not dare to say three, her courage failed her.

He put down the pen and turned towards her in displeasure. "Selina, I told you before we came to town that I could not have these calls made upon me, as I had last year. You know how very small our income is, and you know that your extravagance has already crippled it. The allowance I make you is greater than I can afford. I cannot give you more."

"Oh, Oscar, I must have it," she exclaimed in excitement, terrified at the aspect her situation presented to her, for her mind was apt to be imaginative. "Indeed, I must—even at an inconvenience. But two hundred pounds!"

"To squander away in folly?"

"No. If it were only to squander away, I might do without it; and I cannot do without this."

Mr. Dalrymple looked keenly at her, and she turned from his gaze. " Let me know what you want it for, that I may judge of the necessity you speak of. If it is not convenient to you to tell me, Selina, you must be satisfied with my refusal."

" Well, then," she said, seeing no help for the avowal, " I owe it."

" Owe it! Owe two hundred pounds! *You!*"

So utter was his astonishment, so blank his dismay, that Selina's heart failed her. If her owing two hundred pounds thus impressed him, what would become of her when he learnt the whole truth!

" And I am pressed for it," she faintly added. " *Please* let me have it, Oscar."

" What have you gone in debt for ? "

" Various things," she answered, not caring to avow particulars. But he looked steadfastly at her, waiting for the truth. "Dress."

" The compact between us was that you

should not run in debt," he said, in a severe tone; " you promised to make your allowance do. You have behaved ill to me, Selina."

She bent her head, feeling that she had. Oh, feeling it terribly just then.

" Is this all you owe ? All ? "

" Y—es." But the falsehood, as falsehoods ought to, left a tremor on her lips.

Without speaking another word, he unsealed a paper in which were enclosed some bank notes, and handed several to her, to the amount of two hundred pounds. " Understand me well, Selina, this must never occur again," he said in an impressive tone. " These notes had a different and an urgent destination."

" What a goose I was, not to ask for the other hundred ! " was her mental comment, as she escaped from the room. " It is not of the least use offering Damereau two hundred ; but she might take three. And where am I to get it ? "

Where, indeed ? Did the reader ever try when in extremity to borrow a hundred pounds, or what not ?—and does he remember how very hopeless a case it seemed when present before him? Just as it appeared now to Selina Dalrymple.

"I wonder whether Alice could lend it me?" she cried, swaying her foot helplessly as she sat in the low chair. "It's not in the least likely, but I might ask her.——Who's this?"

The "Who's this," applied to a footstep on the stairs. It was her husband's. Some tiresome, troublesome old man of their acquaintance had come up from Netherleigh, and Oscar wanted his wife to help entertain him. Remembering the two hundred pounds just procured from Oscar, she did not like to refuse, and went down.

They dined, to accommodate this gentleman, at what Selina called an unearthly hour —four o'clock; and it was evening before she could get to Lady Sarah Hope's. Alice, looking ill, was alone in the drawing-room, having begged to be excused going down to dinner. On a table in the back room lay some of Lady Sarah's jewels; valuable gems. Selina privately wished they were hers. She had to take her departure as she came, for Alice could not help her. A curiously mysterious matter connected with these jewels has to be related. It ought to come in here; but it may be better to defer it, not to interfere with the sequence of events pertaining to this chapter.

Nothing further could be done that evening, and Selina went to rest betimes—eleven o'clock—disappointing two or three entertainments that were languishing for her presence: but she had no heart that night.

To rest! It was a mockery of the word, for she had become thoroughly frightened. She passed the night turning and tossing from side to side; and when morning came, and she arose, it was with trembling limbs and a fevered brain.

Her whole anxiety was to make up this money, three hundred pounds; hoping that it would prove a stop-gap for the milliner, and stave off that dreaded threat of application to Oscar. What was to come afterwards, and how in the world further stop-gaps would be supplied, she did not now glance at. That evil seemed a hundred miles off, compared with this.

A faint idea had been looming through her mind; possibly led to by what she had seen at Lady Sarah Hope's. At the commence- ment it had neither shape nor form, but by mid-day it had acquired one, and was enter- tained. She had heard of such things as pledging jewels: she was sure she had heard that even noble ladies, driven to a pinch, so disposed of them. Mrs. Dalrymple locked her bed-room door, reached out her ornaments, and laid them in a heap on the bed.

She began to estimate their value: what they had cost to buy, as nearly as she could remember and judge, amounted to full five hundred pounds. They were not paid for, but that was nothing. She supposed she might be able to borrow four hundred upon them: and she decided to do it. Some few, others, had belonged to her mother. Then, if that cor- morant of a French marchande de modes refused to be pacified with a small sum, she should have a larger one to offer her. Yes, and get the things for the wedding breakfast besides.

The relief this determination brought to the superficial mind of Selina Dalrymple, few, never reduced to a similar strait, can picture. It almost removed her weight of care. The task of pledging them would not be a pleasant one, but she must go through with it. The glittering trinkets were still upon the bed when someone knocked at the room door. It was only her maid, come to say that Miss Alice was below. Selina grew scared and terrified; for a troubled conscience sees shadows where no shadows are, and hers whispered that curious eyes, looking on those ornaments, must divine what she meant to do with them. With a hasty hand she threw a dress upon the bed, and then another upon the first, and then a heavy one over all, before unbolting the door. The glittering jewels were hidden now.

Oscar Dalrymple was thinking profoundly as he sat over his after-dinner wine, not that he ever took much, and the street lamps were lighted, when a figure, looking as little like Mrs. Dalrymple as possible, stole out of the

house ; stole stealthily, and closed the door
stealthily behind her, so that neither master
nor servant should hear it.　She had ransacked
her wardrobe for a plain gown and dark shawl,
and her straw bonnet might have served as a
model for a Quaker's.　She had been out in
the afternoon, and marked the place she
meant to go to.　A renowned establishment
in its line, and respectable, even Selina knew
that.　She hurried along the streets, not
unlike a criminal : had she been going to rob
the warerooms of their jewels, instead of offering some to add to their hidden stock, she
could not have felt more guilty.　When she
reached the place she could not make up her
mind to enter : she took a turn or two in
front, she glanced in at its door, at the window
crowded with goods.　She had never been
in a pawnbroker's shop in her life, and her
ideas of its customers were vague : comprising
gentlewomen in distress, gliding in as she
was ; tipsy men carrying their watches in their
hand ; poor objects out of work, in dilapidated
shirt-sleeves ; and half-starved women with
pillows and flat-irons.　It looked quiet, inside ;

so far as she could see, there did not appear to be a soul. With a desperate effort of resolution she went in.

She stood at the counter, the chief part of the shop being hidden from her. A dark man came forward.

" What can we do for you, ma'am ? "

" Are you the master ? " inquired Selina.

" No."

" I wish to see him."

Another presently appeared : a respectable-looking, well-dressed man, of good manners.

" I am in temporary need of a little money, and wish to borrow some upon my jewels," began Mrs. Dalrymple, in a hoarse whisper ; and she was really so agitated as scarcely to know what she said.

" Are they of value ? " he inquired.

" Some hundreds of pounds. I have them with me."

He requested her to walk into a private room, and placed a chair. She sat down and laid the jewels on the table. He examined them in silence, one after another, not speaking until he had gone through the whole.

"What did you wish to borrow on them?"

"As much as I can," replied Mrs. Dalrymple. "I thought about four hundred pounds."

"Four hundred pounds!" echoed the pawnbroker. "Madam, they are not worth, for this purpose, more than a quarter of the money."

She stared at him in astonishment. "They are real."

"Oh yes. Otherwise, they would not, to us, be worth so many pence."

"Many of them are new within twelve months," urged Selina. "Altogether, they cost more than five hundred pounds."

"To buy. But they are not worth much to pledge. The fashion of these ornaments changes with every season: and that, for one thing, diminishes their value."

"What could you lend me on them?"

"One hundred pounds."

"Absurd!" returned Mrs. Dalrymple, her cheeks flushing. "Why, that one set of amethysts alone cost more. I could not let them go for that. One hundred would be of no use to me."

" Madam, it is entirely at your option, and I assure you I do not press it," he answered, with courteous respect. "We care little about taking these things in ; so many are brought to us now, that our sales are glutted with them."

" You will not be called upon to sell these. I shall redeem them."

The jeweller did not answer. He could have told her that never an article, from a service of gold plate to a pair of boy's boots, was pledged to him yet, but it was quite sure to be redeemed—in intention.

" Are you aware that a great many ladies, even of high degree, now wear false jewellery ? " he resumed.

" No, indeed," she returned. " Neither should I believe it."

" Nevertheless, it is so. And the chief reason is the one I have just mentioned : that in the present day the rage for ornaments is so great, and the fashion of them so continually changing, that to be *in* the fashion, a lady must spend a fortune in ornaments alone. I give you my word, madam, that in the fashionable world a great deal of the jewellery now worn is false ; though it may pass, there, unsuspected. And this fact deteriorates from the value of real stones, especially for the purpose of pledging."

He began, as he spoke, to put the articles into their cases again, as if the negotiation were at an end.

"Can you lend me two hundred pounds upon them ?" asked Mrs. Dalrymple, after a blank pause.

He shook his head. "I can advance you what I have stated, if you please ; not a pound more. And I feel sure you will not be able to obtain more on them anywhere, madam, take them where you will."

"But what am I to do ?" returned she, betraying some excitement. Very uselessly : but that room was no stranger to it.

The jeweller was firm, and Mrs. Dalrymple gathered up her ornaments, her first feeling of despair lost in anger. She was leaving the room with her parcel when it occurred to her to ask herself, in sober truth, WHAT she was to do—how procure the remainder of the sum necessary to appease Madame Damereau. She turned back, and finally left the shop without her jewels, but with a hundred pounds in her pocket, and her understanding considerably enlightened as to the relative value of a jewel to buy and a jewel to pledge.

Now it happened that, if Mrs. Dalrymple had repented showing her temper to Madame Damereau, that renowned artiste had equally repented showing hers to Mrs. Dalrymple. She feared it might tell against her with her customers, if it came to be known: for she knew how popular Selina was: truth to say, she liked her herself. Madame came to the determination of paying Mrs. Dalrymple a visit, not exactly to apologise, but to soothe away certain words. And to qualify the pressing for some money, which she meant to do (whether she got it or not), she intended to announce that the articles ordered for the wedding festivities would be supplied. " It's only ninety pounds, more or less," thought madame, "and I suppose I shall get the money some time."

She reached Mrs. Dalrymple's in the evening, soon after that lady had departed on her secret expedition to the pawnbroker. Their London lodgings were confined. The dining-room had Mr. Dalrymple in it, so Madame Damereau was shown to the drawing-room, and the maid went hunting about the house for her mistress.

Whilst she was on her useless search, Mr. Dalrymple entered the drawing-room, expecting to find it tenanted by his wife. Instead of that, some strange lady sat there, who rose at his entrance, made him a swimming curtsey, the like of which he had never seen in a ball-room, and threw off some rapid sentences in an unknown tongue.

His perplexed look stopped her. "Ah," she said, changing her language, "monsieur, I fear, does not speak the French. I have the honour, I believe, of addressing Mr. Dalreemp. I am covered with contrition at intruding at this evening hour, but I know that Mrs. Dalreemp is much out in the day; I thought I might perhaps get speech of her as she was dressing for some soirée."

"Do you wish to see her? Have you seen her?" asked he.

"I wait now to see her," replied madame.

"Another of these milliner people, I suppose," thought Oscar to himself, with not at all a polite word in connection with the supposition. "Selina's mad to have the house beset with them; it's like a swarm of flies. If she comes to town next year may I be shot!"

"Ann! tell your mistress she is wanted," he called out, opening the door.

"I can't find my mistress, sir," said the servant, coming downstairs. "I thought she must be in her own room, but she is not. I am sure she is not gone out, because she said she meant to have a quiet evening at home to-night, and she did not dress."

"She is somewhere about," said Mr. Dalrymple. "Go and look for her."

Madame Damereau had been coming to the rapid conclusion that this was an opportunity she should do injustice to herself to omit using. And as Mr. Dalrymple was about to leave her to herself, she stopped him.

" Sir—pardon me—but now that I have the happiness to see you, I may ask if you will not use you influence with Mrs. Dalreemp to think of my account. She does promise so often, so often, and I get nothing. I have my heavy payments to make, and sometimes I do not know where to find the money : though, if you saw my books, your hairs would bristle, sir, at the sums owing to me."

" You are —— ?"

" I am Madame Damereau. If Mrs. Dalreemp would but give me a few hundred pounds off her bill, it would be something."

A few hundred pounds ! Oscar Dalrymple wondered what she meant. He looked at her for some moments before he spoke.

" What is the amount of my wife's debt to you, madame ?"

" Ah, it is —— but I cannot tell it you quite exactly : there are recent items. The last note that went in to her was four thousand three hundred and twenty-two pounds."

He had an impassible face, rarely showing

emotion. It had probably not been moved to it half a dozen times in the course of his life. But now his lips gradually drew into a straight thin line, and a red spot shone in his cheek.

"WHAT did you say? Do you speak of the account?"

"It was four thousand three hundred and twenty-two pounds," equably answered madame, who was not familiar with his countenance. "And there have been a few trifles since, and her last order this week will come to ninety pounds. If you wish for it exactly, sir," added madame, seizing at an idea of hope, "I will have it sent to you when I go home. Mrs. Dalreemp has the details up to very recently."

"Four thousand pounds!" repeated Mr. Dalrymple, sitting down, in a sort of helpless manner. "When could she have contracted it?"

"Last season, sir, chiefly. A little in the winter she had sent down to her, and she has had things this spring: not so many."

He did not say more, save a mutter which

madame could not catch. She understood it to be that he would speak to Mrs. Dalrymple: The maid returned, protesting that her mistress was not in the house and must have changed her mind and gone out; and Madame Damereau, thinking she might have gone out for the evening, and that it was of no use waiting, made her adieu to Mr. Dalrymple, with the remarkable curtsey more than once repeated.

He was sitting there still, in the same position, when his wife appeared. She had entered the house stealthily, as she had left it, had taken off her things, and now came into the room ready for tea, as if she had only been upstairs to wash her hands. Scarcely had she reached the middle of the room, when he rose and laid his hand heavily on her shoulder. His face, as she turned to him in alarm, with its drawn aspect, its mingled pallor and hectic, was so changed that she could hardly recognise it for his.

" Oscar, you terrify me !" she cried out.

" What debts are these that you owe ? " he asked, from between his parted lips.

Was the dreaded moment come, then! A low moan escaped her.

"Four thousand and some hundred pounds to Damerean the milliner! How much more to others?"

"Oh, Oscar, if you look and speak like that, you will kill me."

"I ask how much more?" he repeated, passing by her words as the idle wind. "Tell me the truth, or I shall feel tempted to thrust you from my home, and advertise you."

She wished the carpet would open and let her in; she hid her face. Oscar held her, and repeated the question: "How much?"

"Six thousand pounds—in all—about that. Not more, I think."

He released her then with a jerk. Selina began to cry like a school-girl.

"Are you prepared to go out and work for your living, as I must do?" he panted. "I have nothing to keep you on, and shall not have for years. If they throw me into a debtor's prison to-morrow, I cannot help it."

"Oh," shrieked silly Selina, "a prison! I'd go with you."

"I might have expected something of this when I married into your branch of the family," returned Oscar, who, in good truth, was nearly beside himself. "A mania follows it. Your uncle gambled his means away, and then took his own life; your father hampered himself with his brother's debts, and remained poor; your brother followed in his uncle's wake; and now the mania is upon you!"

"Oh, please, Oscar, please!" pleaded Selina, who had no more depth of feeling than a magpie, while Oscar had plenty of it. "I'll never, never go in debt again.'"

"You shall never have the chance," he answered. And, there and then, Oscar Dalrymple, summoning his household, gave orders for their removal to the Grange. Selina cried her eyes out at having to quit the season and its attractions summarily.

Thus, as a wreathing cloud suddenly appears in the sky, and as suddenly fades away, had Mrs. Dalrymple, like a bright vision, appeared to the admiring eyes of the London world, and as suddenly vanished from it.

CHAPTER II.

THE DIAMOND BRACELET.

BUT, as you have heard, there is something yet to tell of that hot June day, or, rather, of its evening, when poor Selina Dalrymple had applied for help, and unsuccessfully, to her sister Alice.

The great world of London was beginning to think of dinner. In a well-furnished dressing-room, the windows being open for air, and the blinds drawn down to exclude the sun, stood a tall, stately lady, whose maid was giving the last touch to her rich attire. It was Lady Sarah Hope.

"What bracelets, my lady?" asked the maid, taking a small bunch of keys from her pocket.

"Not any, now: it is so very hot. Alice," added Lady Sarah, turning to Alice, who was leaning back on a sofa, "will you put all my bracelets out for me against I come up? I will decide then."

"*I* put them out, Lady Sarah?" returned Alice. "Yes, certainly."

"If you will be so kind. Hughes, give the key to Miss Seaton." For they did sometimes remember to address Alice by her adopted name.

Lady Sarah left the room, and the maid, Hughes, began taking one of the small keys off the ring. "I have leave to go out, miss," she explained, "which is the reason why my lady has asked you to see to her bracelets. My mother is not well, and wants to see me. This is the key, ma'am."

As Alice took it, Lady Sarah reappeared at the door. "Alice, you may as well bring the bracelet-box down to the back drawing-room," she said. "I shall not care to come up here after dinner : we shall be late as it is."

"What's that about the bracelet-box?" inquired a pretty-looking girl, who had come swiftly out of another apartment.

"Lady Sarah wishes me to bring her bracelets down to the drawing-room, that she may choose which to put on. It was too hot to wear them to dine in she said."

"Are you not coming in to dinner, Alice ?"

"No. I walked out, and it has tired me. I have had some tea instead."

"I would not be you for all the world, Alice ! To possess so little capability of enjoying life."

"Yet, if you were as I am, weak in health and strength, your lot would have been so soothed to you, Frances, that you would not repine at or regret it."

"You mean I should be content," laughed Frances, upon whom the defection of Mr. Gerard Hope earlier in the year did not appear to have made much impression : though perhaps she did not know its particulars. "Well, there is nothing like contentment, the sages tell us. One of my detestable schoolroom copies used to be 'Contentment is happiness.'"

"I can hear the dinner being taken in," said Alice. "You will be late in the drawing-room."

Lady Frances Chenevix turned away to fly

down the stairs. Her light, rounded form, her elastic step, all telling of health and enjoyment, presented a marked contrast to that of Alice Dalrymple. Alice's face was indeed strangely beautiful, almost too refined and delicate for the wear and tear of common life, but her figure was weak and stooping, and her gait feeble.

Colonel Hope, thin and spare, with sharp brown eyes and sharp features, sat at the foot of his table. He was beginning to look so shrunk and short, that his friends jokingly told him he must have been smuggled into the army, unless he had since been growing downwards, for surely so little a commander could never expect to be obeyed. No stranger could have believed him at ease in his circumstances, any more than they would have believed him a colonel who had seen hard service in India, for his clothes were frequently threadbare. A black ribbon supplied the place of a gold chain as guard to his watch, and a blue, tin-looking thing of a galvanised ring did duty for any other ring on his finger. Yet he was rich; of fabulous riches, people said; but he was of a close disposition, especially as regarded his personal outlay. In his home and to his wife he was liberal. A good husband; and, putting his crustiness and his crotchets aside, a good man. It was the loss of his two boys that had so tried and changed him. His large property was not entailed: it had been thought his nephew, Gerard Hope, would inherit it, but Gerard had been turned from the house. Lady Sarah remarked that it was too hot to dine; but the Colonel, in respect to heat, was a salamander.

Alice meanwhile lay on the sofa for half an hour; and then, taking the bracelet-box in her hands, descended to the drawing-rooms. It was intensely hot, she thought; a sultry, breathless heat; and she threw open the back window. Which in truth made it hotter, for the sun gleamed right athwart the leads which stretched themselves beyond the windows over the outbuildings at the back of the row of houses.

Alice sat down near this back window, and began to put out some of the bracelets on the table before it. They were rare and rich : of plain gold, of silver, of pearl, of precious stones. One of them was of gold links studded with diamonds ; it was very valuable, and had been the present of Colonel Hope to his wife on her recent birthday. Another diamond bracelet was there, but it was not so beautiful or so costly as this. When her task was done, Alice passed into the front drawing-room, and put up one of its large windows. Still there was no air in the room.

As she stood at it, a handsome young man, tall and agile, who was walking on the opposite side of the street, caught her eye. He nodded, hesitated, and then crossed the street as if to enter.

"It is Gerard!" uttered Alice, under her breath. "Can he be coming here ?" She walked away from the window hastily, and sat down by the bedecked table in the other room.

"Just as I supposed!" exclaimed Gerard Hope, entering, and advancing to Alice with stealthy steps. "When I saw you at the window, the thought struck me that you were alone here, and they at dinner. Thomas happened to be airing himself at the door, so I crossed over, found I was right, and came up. How are you, Alice?"

"Have you come to dinner?" inquired Alice, speaking at random, and angry at her own agitation.

"*I* come to dinner!" repeated Gerard. "Why, you know they'd as soon sit down with the renowned Mr. Ketch."

"Indeed I know nothing about it : we have been away in Gloucestershire for months, as I daresay you are aware : I was hoping that you and the Colonel might have been reconciled. Why did you come in, Gerard? Thomas may tell them."

"Thomas won't. I charged him not to. The idea of your never coming up till June ! Some whim of Lady Sarah's, I suppose. Two or three times a week for the last month have I been marching past this house, wondering when it was going to show signs of life. Frances is here still."

"Oh yes. She remains here altogether."

"To make up for —— Alice, was it not a shame to turn me out ? "

"I was extremely sorry for what happened, Mr. Hope, but I knew nothing of the details. Lady Sarah said you had displeased herself and the Colonel, and after that she never mentioned your name."

"What a show of smart things you have here, Alice ! Are you going to set up a bazaar ? "

"They are Lady Sarah's bracelets."

"So they are, I see ! This is a gem," added Mr. Hope, taking up the fine diamond bracelet already mentioned. "I don't remember this one."

"It is new. The Colonel has just given it to her."

"What did it cost ? "

Alice laughed. "Do you think it likely I have heard? I question if Lady Sarah has."

"It never cost a farthing less than two hundred guineas," mused Gerard, turning the bracelet in various directions, that its rich diamonds might give out their gleaming light. "I wish it was mine."

"What should you do with it?" laughed Alice.

"Spout it."

"I do not understand," returned Alice. She really did not.

"I beg your pardon, Alice. I was thinking of the colloquial lingo familiarly applied to such transactions, instead of to whom I was talking. I mean raise money upon it."

"Oh, Mr. Hope!"

"Alice, that's twice you have called me 'Mr. Hope.' I thought I had been 'Gerard' to you for many a year."

"Time changes things; and you seem more like a stranger than you used to," returned Alice, a flush rising to her sensitive face. "But you spoke of raising money : I hope you are not in temporary embarrassment."

"A jolly good thing for me if it turns out only temporary," he rejoined. "Look at my position! Debts hanging over my head—for you may be sure, Alice, all young men, with a limited allowance and large expectations, contract debts—and thrust out of my uncle's

home with just the loose cash I had in my
pocket, and my clothes sent packing after
me."

"Has the Colonel stopped your allowance?"

Gerard Hope laid down the bracelet from
whence he had taken it, before he replied.

"He stopped it then; it's months ago, you
know; and I have not had a shilling since,
except from my own resources. I first went
upon tick; then I disposed of my watch and
chain and all my other little matters of value:
and now I am upon tick again."

Alice did not answer. The light tone
vexed her.

"Perhaps you don't understand these free
terms, Alice," he said, looking fondly at her,
"and I hope you may never have occasion
to. Frances would: she has lived in their
atmosphere."

"Yes, I know what an embarrassed man
the Earl often is. But I am grieved to hear
about yourself. Is the Colonel implacable?
What was the cause of the quarrel?"

"You know I was to be his heir. Even if
more children had come to him, he undertook

to provide amply for me. Last autumn he suddenly sent for me, and told me it was his pleasure and Lady Sarah's that I should take up my abode with them. So I did take it up, glad to get into such good quarters; and stopped here, like an innocent, unsuspicious lamb, until—when was it, Alice?—March? Then the plot came out."

"The plot?" exclaimed Alice.

"It was nothing less. They had fixed upon a wife for me; and I was ordered to hold myself in readiness to marry her at any given moment."

"Who was it?" inquired Alice, in a low tone, as she bent her head over the bracelets.

"Never mind," laughed the young man; "it wasn't you. I said I would not have her; and they both, he and Lady Sarah, pulled me and my want of taste to pieces, assuring me I was a monster of ingratitude. It provoked me into confessing that I liked somebody else better. And then the Colonel turned me out."

Alice looked her sorrow, but she did not express it.

"Of course I saw the imprudence then of having thrown up my place in the Red-tape Office ; but it was done. And since then I have been having a fight with my creditors, putting them off with fair words and promises. But they have grown incredulous, and it has come to dodging. In favour with my uncle, and his acknowledged heir, they would have given me unlimited time and credit, but the breach between us is known, and it makes all the difference. With the value of that at my disposal" — nodding at the bracelet — "I should stop a few pressing personal trifles and go on again for a while. So you see, Alice, a diamond bracelet may be of use even to a gentleman, should some genial fortune drop one into his hands."

"I sympathise with you very much," said Alice, "and I would I had it in my power to aid you."

"Thank you for your kind wishes ; I know they are genuine. When my uncle sees the name of Gerard Hope figuring in the insolvent list, or amongst the outlaws, he —— Hark! Can they be coming up from dinner?"

" Scarcely yet," said Alice, starting up simultaneously with himself, and listening. " But they will not sit long to-day, because they are going to the opera. Gerard, they must not find you here."

" It might get you turned out as well as myself! No, not if I can help it! Alice ! " suddenly laying his hands upon her shoulders, and gazing down into her eyes—" do you know who it was I had learnt to love, instead of—of the other ?"

She gasped for breath, and her colour went and came. " No — no; do not tell me, Gerard."

" Why, no, I had better not, under present circumstances. But when the good time comes—for all their high-roped indignation must and will blow over—*then I will;* and here's the pledge of it." He bent his head, took one long earnest kiss from her lips ; and the next moment was gone.

Agitated almost to sickness, trembling and confused, Alice stole to look after him, terri-fied lest he might not escape unseen. She crept partly down the stairs, so as to obtain

sight of the hall-door, and make sure that he
got out in safety. As Gerard drew it quietly
open, there stood a lady just about to knock.
It was Selina. Waiting to exchange a few
words with Gerard, he waved his hand towards the staircase. Alice met her, and took
her into the front drawing-room.

"I cannot stay to sit down, Alice; I must
make haste back to dress, for I am engaged
to three or four places to-night. Neither do
I wish to horrify Lady Sarah with a visit at
this untoward hour. I had a request to make
to you, and thought to catch you in your
room before you went in to dinner."

"They are alone, and are dining earlier
than usual. I was too tired to appear. What
can I do for you, Selina?"

Mrs. Oscar Dalrymple had come (as you
have already heard) to try that one hopeless task—the borrowing money of her
sister.

"I am in pressing need of it, Alice," she
said. "Can you lend it me?"

"I wish I could," returned Alice; "I am
so very sorry. I sent all I had to poor

mamma the day before we came to town. It was only twenty-five pounds."

"*That* would have been of no use to me: I want more. I thought if you had been misering up your salary, you might have had a hundred pounds, or so, by you."

Alice shook her head. "I should be a long while saving up a hundred pounds, even if dear mamma had no wants. But I send to her what I can spare. Is it for—dresses, and that ? "

" Yes," was Selina's laconic answer.

" I wish I had it to give you !——Do not be in such a hurry," continued Alice, as her sister was moving to the door. " At least wait one minute while I fetch you a letter I received from mamma this morning, in answer to mine. You will like to read it, for it is full of news of the old place. You can take it home with you, Selina."

Alice left her sister standing in the front room, and went up-stairs. But she was more than one minute away, she was three or four, for she could not at first lay her hand upon the letter. When she returned, her sister advanced to her from the back drawing-room, the folding-doors between the two rooms being, as before, wide open.

" What a fine collection of bracelets, Alice !" she exclaimed, as she took the letter. " Are they spread out for show ?"

" No," laughed Alice ; " Lady Sarah is going to the opera, and will have no time to spare when she comes up from dinner. She asked me to bring them all down, as she had not decided which to wear."

" I like to dress entirely before dinner on my opera nights."

" Oh, so of course does Lady Sarah," returned Alice, as her sister descended the stairs ; " but she said it was too hot to dine in bracelets."

" It is fearfully hot. Good-bye, Alice. Don't ring : I will let myself out."

Alice returned to the front room and looked from the window, wondering whether her sister had come in her carriage. No. A trifling evening breeze was arising and beginning to move the curtains about. Gentle as it was, it was grateful, and Alice sat down in it. In a very few minutes the ladies came up from dinner.

"Have you the bracelets, Alice. Oh, I see."

Lady Sarah went into the back room as she spoke, and stood before the table, looking at the bracelets. Alice rose to follow her, when Lady Frances Chenevix caught her by the arm, and began to speak in a covert whisper.

"Who was that at the door just now ? It was a visitor's knock. Do you know, Alice, every hour, since we came to town, I have fancied Gerard might be calling. In the country he could not get to us, but here— Was it Gerard ?"

"It—it was my sister," carelessly answered Alice. It was not a true answer, for her sister had not knocked, and she did not know who had. But it was the readiest that rose to her lips, and she wished to escape the questioning, for more reasons than one.

"Only your sister," replied Frances, turning to the window with a gesture of disappointment.

"Which have you put on?" inquired Alice, going towards Lady Sarah.

"These loose, fancy things; they are the coolest. I really am so hot: the soup was that favourite soup of the Colonel's, all capsicums and cayenne, and the wine was hot; there had been a mistake about the ice. Gill trusted to the new man, and he did not understand it; it was all hot together. What the house will be to-night, I dread to think of."

Lady Sarah, whilst she spoke, had been putting the bracelets into the jewel-box, with very little care.

"I had better put them straight," remarked Alice, when she reached the table.

"Do not trouble," returned Lady Sarah, shutting down the lid. "You are looking flushed and feverish, Alice; you were wrong to walk so far to-day. Hughes will set them to rights to-morrow morning; they will do until then. Lock them up, and take possession of the key."

Alice did as she was bid. She locked the case and put the key in her pocket. "Here is the carriage," exclaimed Lady Frances. "Are we to wait for coffee?"

"Coffee in this heat!" retorted Lady Sarah; "it would be adding fuel to fire. We will have some tea when we return. Alice, you must make tea for the Colonel; he will not come out without it. He thinks this weather just what it ought to be: rather cold, if anything."

Alice had taken the bracelet-box in her hands as Lady Sarah spoke; when they had departed she carried it up-stairs to its place in Lady Sarah's bed-room. The Colonel speedily rose from table, for his wife had laid her commands on him to join them early. Alice helped him to his tea, and as soon as he was gone she went up-stairs to bed.

To bed, but not to sleep. Tired as she was, and exhausted in frame, sleep would not come to her. She was living over again her interview with Gerard Hope. She could not, in her conscious heart, affect to misunderstand his implied meaning—that *she* had been the cause of his rejecting the union proposed to him. It diffused a strange rapture within her; and, though she had not perhaps been wholly blind and unconscious during the period of Gerard's stay with them, and for some time before that, she now kept repeating the words, " Can it be that he loves me ? can it be ? "

It certainly was so. Love plays strange pranks. There was Gerard Hope—heir to the Colonel's fabulous wealth, consciously proud of his handsome person, his height and strength—called home and planted down by the side of a pretty and noble lady, on purpose that he might fall in love with her: the Lady Frances Chenevix. And yet, the well-laid project failed : failed because there happened to be another at that young lady's side : a sad, quiet, feeble-framed girl, whose very weakness may have seemed to others to place her beyond the pale of man's love. But love thrives by contrasts; and it was the feeble girl who won the love of the strong man.

Yes; the knowledge diffused a strange rapture within her, Alice Dalrymple, as she lay there that night; and she may be excused if, for a brief period, she allowed range to the sweet fantasies it conjured up. For a brief period only. Too soon the depressing consciousness returned to her, that these thoughts of earthly happiness must be subdued; for she, with her confirmed ailments and conspicuous weakness, must never hope to marry, as did other women. She had long known— her mother had prepared her for it—that one so afflicted and frail as she, whose tenure of existence was likely to be short, ought not to become a wife ; and it had been her earnest hope to pass through life unloving, in that one sense, and unloved. She had striven to arm herself against the danger, against being thrown into the perils of temptation. Alas ! it had come insidiously upon her ; all her care had been set at naught; and she knew that she loved Gerard Hope with a deep and fervent love. " It is but another cross," she sighed, " another burden to surmount and subdue, and I will set myself from this night to the task. I have been a coward, shrinking from self-examination ; but now that Gerard has spoken out, I can deceive myself no longer. I wish he had spoken more freely, that I might have told him it was useless."

It was only towards morning that Alice dropped asleep : the consequence was, that long after her usual hour for rising she was still sleeping. The opening of her door awoke her. It was Lady Sarah's maid who stood there.

"Why, miss ! are you not up ? Well, I never ! I wanted the key of the small jewel-box, but I'd have waited had I known."

"What do you say you want ?" returned Alice, whose ideas were confused ; as is often the case on being suddenly awakened.

"The key of the bracelet-box, if you please."

"The key ?" repeated Alice. "Oh, I remember," she added, her recollection returning to her. "Be at the trouble, will you, Hughes, to take it out of my pocket : it is on that chair, under my clothes."

The servant came to the pocket, and speedily found the key "Are you worse than usual, Miss Seaton, this morning," asked she, "or have you overslept yourself ?"

" I have overslept myself.   Is it late ?"

" Between nine and ten.   My lady is up,
and at breakfast with the Colonel and Lady
Frances."

Alice rose the instant the maid left the
room, and made haste to dress, vexed with
herself for sleeping so long.   She was nearly
ready when Hughes came in again.

" If ever I saw such confusion as that
jewel-case was in ! " cried she, in as pert and
grumbling a tone as she dared to use.   " The
bracelets were thrown together without law or
order—just as if they had been so much glass
and tinsel from the Lowther Arcade."

" It was Lady Sarah," replied Alice.   " I
would have put them straight, but she told
me to leave it for you.   I thought she might
prefer that you should do it."

" Of course her ladyship is aware there's
nobody but myself knows their right places in
it," returned Hughes, consequentially.   " I
could go to that or to the other jewel-box in
the dark, ma'am, and take out any one thing
my lady wanted, without disturbing the rest."

" I have observed that you have the gift of

order," remarked Alice, with a smile. " It is very useful to those who possess it, and saves them much trouble and confusion."

" So it do, ma'am," said Hughes. " But I came to ask you for the diamond bracelet."

" The diamond bracelet!" echoed Alice. " What diamond bracelet? What do you mean, Hughes?"

" It is not in the box."

" The diamond bracelets are both in the box," rejoined Alice.

" The old one is there ; not the new one. I thought you might have taken it out to show some one, or to look at yourself, ma'am, for it's just a sight for pleasant eyes."

" I can assure you it is in the case," said Alice. " All are there except the pair Lady Sarah had on. You must have overlooked it."

" I am a great donkey if I have," grumbled the girl. " It must be at the very bottom, amongst the cotton," she soliloquised, as she returned to Lady Sarah's apartments, " and I have just got to take every individual article out, to get to it. This comes of giving up one's keys to other folks."

Alice entered the breakfast-room, begging
pardon for her late appearance. It was
readily accorded. Her office in the house was
nearly a sinecure. When she had first entered upon it Lady Sarah was ill, and required
some one to sit with and read to her : now
that she was well again Alice had little to do.

Breakfast was scarcely over when Alice
was called from the room. Hughes stood
outside the door.

"Miss Seaton," said she, with a long face,
"the diamond bracelet is not in the box. I
thought I could not be mistaken."

"But it must be in the box," said Alice.

"But it is *not*," persisted Hughes, em-
phasising the negative. "Can't you believe
me, ma'am ? I want to know where it is, that
I may put it up and lock the box."

Alice Seaton looked at Hughes with a
puzzled, dreamy look. She was thinking
matters over. Her face soon cleared again.

"Then Lady Sarah must have kept it out
when she put in the rest. It was she who
returned them to the case ; I did not. Perhaps
she wore it last night."

"No, miss, that she didn't. She wore only those two ——"

"I saw what she had on," interrupted Alice. "But she might also have put on the other, without my noticing. Or she may have kept it out for some other purpose. I will ask her. Wait here an instant, Hughes; for of course you will like to be at a certainty."

"That's cool," thought Hughes, as Alice went into the breakfast-room, and the Colonel came out of it, with his *Times*. "I should have said it was somebody else would like to be at a certainty, instead of me," continued the girl, indulging in self-soliloquy. "Thank goodness the box wasn't in my charge last night, if anything dreadful has come to pass. My lady don't keep out her bracelets for sport. Miss Seaton has left the key about, that's what she has done, and it's hard to say who hasn't been at it: I knew the box had been ransacked over."

"Lady Sarah," said Alice, "did you wear your new diamond bracelet last night?"

"No."

"Then you put it into the box with the others!"

"No," repeated Lady Sarah, who was languidly toying with a basket of ferns.

"After you had chosen the bracelets you wished to wear, you put the others into the box yourself," explained Alice, thinking she was not understood. "Did you put in the new one, the diamond, or keep it out?"

"The new one was not there."

Alice stood confounded. "It was lying on the table, at the back of all the rest, Lady Sarah," she presently said. "Next the window."

"I tell you, Alice, it was not there. I don't know that I should have worn it if it had been, but I certainly looked for it. Not seeing it, I supposed you had not put it out; and I did not care sufficiently to ask for it."

Alice felt in a mesh of perplexity; curious thoughts, and very unpleasing ones, were beginning to dawn upon her. "But indeed the bracelet was there when you went to the table," she urged. "I put it there."

"I can assure you that you labour under a

mistake, as to its being there when I came up from dinner," answered Lady Sarah. " Why do you ask ? "

" Hughes has come to say it is not in the case. She is outside, waiting."

" Outside, now ? Let her come in.— What's this about my bracelet, Hughes ? "

" *I* don't know, my lady. The bracelet is not in its place, so I asked Miss Seaton for it. She thought your ladyship might have kept it out yesterday evening."

" I neither touched it nor saw it," said Lady Sarah.

" Then we have had thieves at work," spoke Hughes, decisively ; who had been making up her mind to that as a fact.

" It must be in the box, Hughes," said Alice. " I laid it out on the table in the back drawing-room ; and it is impossible that thieves—as you phrase it—could have come there."

" Oh, yes, it is in the box, no doubt," said Lady Sarah, somewhat crossly, for she disliked to be troubled, especially in hot weather. " You have not searched properly, Hughes."

"My lady," answered Hughes, "I can trust my hands and I can trust my eyes, and they have all four been into every hole and crevice of the box."

Lady Frances Chenevix laid down the *Morning Post*, and advanced. "Is the bracelet really lost?"

"It cannot be lost," returned Lady Sarah. "You are sure you put it out, Alice?"

"I am quite sure of that. It was lying first in the case, and ——"

"Yes it was," interrupted Hughes. "That is its place."

"And was consequently the first that I took out," continued Alice. "I put it on the table; and the others in a semicircle, nearer to me. Why, as a proof that it lay there ——"

What was Alice going to add? Was she going to adduce as a proof that Gerard Hope had taken it up and made it a subject of conversation? Recollection came to her in time; she faltered, and abruptly broke off. But a faint, horrible dread, to which she would not give a shape, came stealing over her, and her face turned white, and she sank on a chair, trembling visibly.

"Now look at Alice!" uttered Frances Chenevix. "She is going into one of her agitation fits."

"Do not agitate yourself, Alice," cried Lady Sarah; "that will do no good. Besides, I feel sure the bracelet is all safe in the case: where else can it be? Fetch the case, Hughes, and I will look for it myself."

Hughes whisked out of the room, inwardly resenting the doubt cast on her eyesight.

"It is so strange," mused Alice, "that you did not see the bracelet when you came up from dinner."

"It was certainly not there to see," returned Lady Sarah.

"Perhaps you'll now look for yourself, my lady," cried Hughes, returning with the jewel-box in her hands.

The box was well searched. The bracelet was not there.

"This is very strange, Hughes," exclaimed Lady Sarah.

"It's very ugly as well, my lady," answered

Hughes, in a lofty tone, "and I'm thankful to the presiding genuses which rules such things, that I was not in charge when it happened. Though maybe, if I had been, it never would have took place, for I can give a guess how it was."

"Then you had better give it," said her mistress, curtly.

"If I do," returned Hughes, "I may offend Miss Seaton."

"No, you will not, Hughes," said Alice. "Say what you please: I have need to wish this cleared up."

"Then, ma'am, if I may speak my thoughts, I think you must have left the key about. And there are strange servants in the house, as my lady knows. There's a kitchen-maid that only entered it when we came up; and there's the new under-butler."

"Hughes, you are wrong," interrupted Alice. "The servants could not have touched the box, for the key was never out of my possession, and you know the lock is a Bramah. I locked the box last night in Lady Sarah's presence, and the key was not out of my pocket afterwards, until you took it from thence this morning."

"The key seems to have had nothing to do with it," interposed Frances. "Alice says she put the diamond bracelet on the table with the rest; Lady Sarah says when she went to the table after dinner, the bracelet was not there. Were you in the room all the while, Alice?"

"Not quite. Very nearly. But no one could possibly have gone in without my seeing them. The folding-doors were open."

"It is quite a mystery," cried Lady Sarah.

"It beats conjuring, my lady," said Hughes. "Did any visitor come up-stairs, I wonder?"

"I did hear a visitor's knock while we were at dinner," said Lady Sarah. "Don't you remember, Fanny? You looked up as if you noticed it."

"Did I?" answered Lady Frances, in a careless tone.

At that moment Thomas happened to enter with a letter, and his mistress put the question to him. Who had knocked?

"Sir George Danvers, my lady," was the ready answer. "When I said the Colonel was at dinner, Sir George began to apologise for calling; but I explained that you were dining earlier than usual, because of the opera."

"Nobody else called?"

"Nobody knocked but Sir George, my lady."

"A covert answer," thought Alice. "But I am glad he is true to Gerard."

"What an untruth!" thought Lady Frances, as she remembered hearing of the visit of Alice's sister. "Thomas's memory must be short." In point of fact, Thomas knew nothing of it.

All the talk—and it was much prolonged —did not tend to throw any light upon the matter; and Alice, unhappy and ill, retired to her own room. The agitation had brought on a nervous and violent headache; she sat down in a low chair, and bent her forehead on her hands. One belief alone possessed her: that the unfortunate Gerard Hope had stolen the bracelet. Do as she would, she could not put it out of her mind: she kept repeating that he was a gentleman, that he was honourable, that he would never place her in so painful a position. Common sense replied that the temptation was suddenly laid before him, and he had confessed his pecuniary difficulties to be great: nay, had he not wished for this very bracelet, that he might make money ——

A knock at the chamber door. Alice lifted her sickly countenance, and bade the intruder enter. It was Lady Frances Chenevix.

"I came to —— Alice, how wretched you look! You will torment yourself into a fever."

"Can you wonder at my looking wretched?" returned Alice. "Place yourself in my position, Frances: it must appear to Lady Sarah as if I—I—had made away with the bracelet. I am sure Hughes thinks so."

"Don't you say unorthodox things, Alice. They would rather think that I had done it, of the two, for I have more use for diamond bracelets than you."

"It is kind of you to try to cheer me," sighed Alice.

"Just the thing I came to do. And to have a bit of chat with you as well. If you will let me."

" Of course I will let you."

" I wish to tell you I will not mention that your sister was here last evening. I promise you I will not."

Alice did not immediately reply. The words and their hushed tone caused a new trouble, a fresh thought, to arise within her, one which she had not glanced at. Was it possible that Frances could imagine her sister to be the ——

"Lady Frances Chenevix!" burst forth Alice. " You cannot think it! She! my sister—guilty of a despicable theft! Have you forgotten that she moves in your own position in the world? that our family is scarcely inferior to yours?"

" Alice, I forgive you for so misjudging me because you are not yourself just now. Of course, your sister cannot be suspected; I know that. But as you did not mention her when they were questioning Thomas, nor did he, I supposed you had some reason for not wishing her visit spoken of."

"Believe me, Selina is not the guilty person," returned Alice. "I have more cause to say so than you think for."

"What do you mean by that?" briskly cried Lady Frances. "You surely have no clue?"

Alice shook her head, and her companion's eagerness was lulled again. "It is well that Thomas was forgetful," remarked Frances.

"Was it forgetfulness, Alice; or did you contrive to telegraph to him to be silent?"

"Thomas only spoke truth, as regards Selina: he did not let her in. She came but for a minute, to ask me about a private matter, and said there was no need to tell Lady Sarah she had been."

"Then it is all quite easy; and you and I can keep our own counsel."

Quite easy, possibly, to the mind of Frances Chenevix. But anything but easy to Alice Dalrymple: for the words of Lady Frances had introduced an idea more repulsive, more terrifying even, than that of suspecting Gerard

Hope. Her sister acknowledged that she was in need of money, " a hundred pounds, or so," nay, Alice had only too good cause to know that previously, and she had seen her coming from the back room where the jewels lay. Still—*she* take a bracelet! Selina! It was preposterous.

Preposterous or not, Alice's torment was doubled. Which of the two had been the black sheep? One of them it must have been. Instinct, sisterly relationship, reason, and common sense, all combined to turn the scale against Gerard. But that there should be a doubt at all was not pleasant, and Alice started up impulsively and put her bonnet on.

" Where now! " cried Lady Frances.

" I will go to Selina's and ask her—and ask her—if—she saw any stranger here—any suspicious person in the hall or on the stairs," stammered Alice, making the best excuse she could make.

" But you know you were in or about the drawing-rooms all the time, and no one came into them, suspicious or unsuspicious ; so, how will that aid you ?"

"True," murmured Alice. "But it will be a relief to go somewhere or do something."

Alice found her sister at home: had disturbed her, in fact, at a very interesting employment, as the reader may remember. In spite of her own emotional preoccupation, Selina instantly detected that something was wrong; for the suspense, illness, and agitation had taken every vestige of colour from Alice's cheeks and lips.

"What can be the matter, Alice?" was her greeting. "You look just like a walking ghost."

"I feel that I do," breathed poor Alice, "and I kept my veil down in the street, lest I might be taken for one and scare the people. A great misfortune has fallen upon me, Selina. You saw those bracelets last night, spread out on the table?"

"Yes."

"They were in my charge, and one of them has been abstracted. It was of great value: gold links, holding diamonds."

"Abstracted!" repeated the elder sister, in both concern and surprise, but certainly without the smallest indications of a guilty knowledge. "How? In what manner?"

"It is a mystery. I only left the room when I met you on the staircase, and when I went up-stairs to fetch the letter for you. Directly after you left, Lady Sarah came up from dinner, and the bracelet was not there."

"It is incredible, Alice. And no one else entered the room at all, you say? No servant? no ——"

"Not anyone," interrupted Alice, determined not to speak of Gerard Hope.

"Then, child, it is simply impossible," was the calm rejoinder. "It must have fallen on the ground; or been mislaid in some way."

"It is hopelessly gone. Do you remember seeing it?"

"I do remember seeing amidst the rest a bracelet set with diamonds; but only on the clasp, I think. It ——"

"That was another; that one is all safe," interrupted Alice. "The one missing is of fine gold links interspersed with brilliants. Did you see it?"

"Not that I remember. I was there scarcely a minute, for I had only strolled into the back room just before you came down. To tell you the truth, Alice, my mind was too fully occupied with other things, to take much notice even of jewels. Do not look so perplexed: it will be all right. Only you and I were in the room, you say; and we could not take it."

"Oh!" exclaimed Alice, clasping her hands, and lifting her white, beseeching face to her sister's, "did you take it? In—in sport; or in —— Oh, surely you were not tempted to take it for anything else? Forgive me, Selina! you said you had need of money."

"Alice, are we going to have one of your old scenes of excitement? Strive for calmness. I am sure you do not know what you are implying. My poor child, I would rather help you to jewels than take them from you."

"But look at the mystery."

"It does appear to be a mystery, but it will no doubt be cleared up," was the reply, calm and equable. "Alice, what could you

have been dreaming of, to suspect me ? Have
we not grown up together in our honourable
home ? You ought to know me, if anyone
does."

"And you really saw nothing of it !"
moaned Alice, with a sobbing catching of the
breath.

" Indeed I did not. In truth, I did not.
If I could help you out of your perplexity I
would thankfully do it. Shall I return with
you and assist you to search for the bracelet ? "

" No, thank you. Every search has been
made."

" You have not told me what could induce
you to suspect me ?"

" I think—it was the impossibility of suspecting anybody else," breathed poor Alice,
with hesitation. "And you told me, you
know, Selina, how very badly you wanted
money."

" So I do ; far more badly than you have
any idea of, child. So badly that the thought
crossed me for a moment of applying to that
dreadfully rich fifteenth cousin of papa's in

Liverpool, Benjamin Dalrymple, who estranged himself from us years ago; but I knew he would only growl out a No if I did apply. But not badly enough, Alice, to bring me to the stealing of a diamond bracelet," emphatically concluded Selina.

Not only was the denial fervent and calm, but Selina's manner and countenance conveyed the impression of truth. Alice left her, inexpressibly relieved; though the conviction, that it must have been Gerard, returned to her in full force. "I wish I could see him!" was her mental exclamation.

And for once fortune favoured her wish. As she was dragging her weary limbs along, he came right upon her at the corner of a street.

"I am so thankful," she exclaimed. "I wanted to see you."

"I think you most want to see a doctor, Alice. How ill you look!"

"I have cause," she returned. "That bracelet has been stolen."

"Which bracelet?" asked Gerard.

"That valuable one. The diamond. It was taken from the room."

" Taken when ? " he rejoined, looking her full in the face—as a guilty man would scarcely dare to look."

"Then; or within a few minutes of that time. When Lady Sarah came up from dinner it was not there. She came up almost immediately."

" Who took it ? " he repeated, not yet re-covering his surprise.

"I don't know," she faintly said. "It was under my charge. No one else was there."

" You do not wish me to understand that *you* are suspected," he burst forth with genuine feeling. " Their unjust meanness cannot have gone that length."

" I trust not, but I am very unhappy. It is true I left the room when you did, but I only lingered outside on the stairs, watching —if I may tell the truth—whether you got out safely, and then I returned to it. Yet when Lady Sarah came up from dinner it was gone."

" And did no one else go into the room ? " he repeated. "Did Selina ? I met her at the door, and sent her up-stairs."

" She went in for a minute. But she would not touch the jewels, Gerard."

" Of course not. She counts as ourselves in this. The bracelet was in the room when I left it —— "

" You are sure of that?" interrupted Alice,

" I am. When I reached the door, I turned round to take a last look at you, and the diamonds of that particular bracelet gleamed at me from its place on the table."

" Oh, Gerard ! Is this the truth ? "

" It is the truth, on my sacred word of honour," he replied, looking at her agitated face and wondering at her words. " Why else should I say it ? Good-bye, Alice ; I cannot stay another moment, for there's somebody yonder I don't want to meet."

He was off like a shot. But his words and manner had conveyed a conviction of innocence to the mind of Alice, just as those of her sister had done. She stood still, looking after him in her dreamy wonder, and was jostled by the passers-by, mentally asking herself *which* of the two was the real delinquent? One of them it must have been.

CHAPTER III.

DRIVEN INTO EXILE.

COLONEL HOPE was striding about his library with impatient steps. He wore a wadded dressing-gown, handsome once, but remarkably shabby now, and he wrapt it closely round him, though the heat of the weather was intense. But Colonel Hope, large as were his coffers, never spent upon himself a superfluous farthing, especially in the way of personal adornment; and Colonel Hope would not have felt too warm cased in sheepskins, for he had spent the best part of his life in India, and was, besides, of a chilly nature.

That same afternoon he had been made acquainted with the unpleasant transaction which had occurred in his house the past evening. The household termed it a mystery; he, a scandalous robbery: and he had written forthwith to the nearest chief police-station, demanding that an officer might be despatched back with the messenger, to investigate it. So there he was, waiting for their return in impatient expectation, and occasionally halting before the window, to look out on the busy London world.

The officer at length came, and was introduced. Lady Sarah joined them, and she proceeded to give him the outline of the case. A valuable diamond bracelet, recently presented to Lady Sarah by her husband, had disappeared in a singular manner. Miss Seaton Dalrymple, the companion to Lady Sarah, had temporary charge of the jewel-box. She had brought it down the previous evening, Thursday, this being Friday, to the back drawing-room, and laid several pairs of bracelets out on a table, ready for Lady Sarah, who was going to the opera, to choose which she would wear when she came up from dinner. Lady Sarah chose a pair, and put, herself, the rest back into the box, which Miss Seaton then locked, and carried to its place upstairs. In the few minutes that the bracelets lay on the table, the most valuable one of all, a diamond, disappeared from it.

"I did not want this to be officially investigated; at least, not so quickly," observed Lady Sarah to the officer. "The Colonel wrote for you quite against my wish."

"And so have let the thief get clear off, and put up with the loss!" cried the Colonel. "Very fine, my lady."

"You see," added her ladyship, explaining to the officer, "Miss Dalrymple is a young lady of extremely good family, with whom we are intimate. She is of feeble constitution, and this affair has so completely upset her, that I fear she will be laid on a sick-bed."

"It won't be my fault, if she is," retorted the Colonel, taking the implied reproach to himself. "She'd be as glad to find it out as ourselves. The loss of a diamond bracelet, worth two or three hundred guineas, is not to be hushed up. They are not to be bought every day, Lady Sarah."

The officer was taken to the back drawing-room whence the bracelet disappeared. It presented nothing peculiar. The folding-doors

between it and the front room stood open, the
back window, a large one, looked out upon
some flat leads. He seemed to take in the
points of the double room at a glance : he
examined the latches of the two doors opening
to the corridor, he looked next from the front
windows, and then from the one at the back.
From the front ones ordinary ingress was impossible ; it was nearly as much so from the
back one. The officer leaned out for some
time, but could make nothing of a case. The
window was shut in by a balcony that just
encircled it, and was not accessible from
the leads underneath. The house was one
of a row of houses, or terrace, and they all
bore the same features : the leads running
along below ; the confining balconies to the
windows on this floor above. But the windows could not be gained from the leads
except by means of a ladder ; and the balconies were not near each other.

"Nothing to be suspected there," concluded the officer, bringing in his head and
shoulders. "I should like, if you please,
ma'am, to see Miss Dalrymple."

Lady Sarah went for her, and brought her. A delicate girl with a transparent skin, looking almost too weak to walk. She was in a visible tremor, and shook as she stood before the police officer : whose name, it turned out, was Pullet.

But he was a man of pleasant manners and speech, and he hastened to reassure her. "There's nothing to be afraid of, young lady," said he, with a broad smile. "We are not ogres : though I do believe some timid folks look upon us as such. Just please to compose yourself, and tell me as much as you can recollect of this."

"I laid out the bracelets here," began Alice, indicating the table underneath the window. "The diamond bracelet, the one lost, I placed just here," she added, touching the middle of the table at the back, "and the rest I put around it."

"It was worth more than any of the others, I believe, ma'am."

"Much more," growled the Colonel.

The officer nodded to himself, and Alice resumed.

"I left the bracelets, and went into the other room and sat down at one of the front windows ——"

"With the intervening doors open, I presume."

"Wide open, as they are now," said Alice. "The other two doors were shut. Lady Sarah came up from dinner almost directly; and then, as it appears, the bracelet was not there."

"You are quite certain of that?"

"*I* am quite certain," interposed Lady Sarah. "I looked particularly for that bracelet; not seeing it, I supposed Miss Seaton had not laid it out. I chose out a pair, put them on, returned the others to the box, and saw Miss Dalrymple lock it."

"Then your ladyship did not miss the bracelet at that time?" questioned Mr. Pullet.

"I did not miss it in one sense, because I did not know it had been put out," she returned. "I saw it was not there."

"But did you not miss it?" he asked of Alice.

"I only reached the table as Lady Sarah

was closing the lid of the box," she answered. " Lady Frances Chenevix had detained me in the front room."

" My sister," explained Lady Sarah. " She is staying with me, and had come up with me from dinner."

" You say you went and sat in the front room," resumed the officer to Alice, in a quicker tone than he had used previously ; " will you show me where ?"

Alice did not stir ; she only turned her head towards the front room, and pointed to a chair a little drawn away from the window. " In that chair," she said. " It stood as it stands now."

The officer looked baffled. " You must have had the back room full in view from thence ; both the door and window."

" Quite so," replied Alice. " If you will sit down in it, you will perceive that I had an uninterrupted view, and faced the doors of both rooms."

" I perceive that from here. And you saw no one enter !"

" No one did enter. It was impossible

anyone could do so, without my observing it. Had either of the doors been only quietly un- latched, I must have both heard and seen."

" And yet the bracelet vanished !" inter- posed Colonel Hope. " They must have been confoundedly deep whoever did it; but thieves are said to possess sleight of hand."

" They are clever enough, some of them," observed the officer.

" Rascally villains ! I should like to know how they accomplished this."

" So should I," significantly returned the officer. " At present it appears to me incom- prehensible."

There was a pause; the officer seemed to muse, and Alice, happening to look up, saw his eyes stealthily studying her face. It did not tend to reassure her.

" Your servants are trustworthy; they have lived with you some time ?" resumed Mr. Pullet, not apparently attaching much importance to what the answer might be.

" Were they all escaped convicts, I don't see that it would throw light on this," re- torted Colonel Hope. " If they came into the room to steal the bracelet, Miss Dalrymple must have seen them."

"From the time you put out the bracelets, to that of the ladies coming up from dinner, how long was it?" inquired the officer of Alice.

"I scarcely know," panted she. What with his close looks and his close questions, her breath was growing short. "I did not take particular notice of the lapse of time: I was not well yesterday evening."

"Was it half an hour?"

"Yes—I daresay—nearly so."

"Miss Dalrymple," he continued, in a brisk tone, "will you have any objection to take an oath before a magistrate—in private, you know—that no person whatever, except yourself, entered either of these rooms during that period?"

Had she been requested to go before a magistrate to testify that she, herself, was the guilty person, it could scarcely have affected her more. Her cheeks grew white, her lips parted, and her eyes assumed a beseeching look of terror. Lady Sarah Hope hastily pushed a chair behind her, and drew her down upon it.

"Really, Alice, you are very foolish to allow yourself to be excited about nothing," she remonstrated : "you would have fallen on the floor in another minute. What l arm is there in taking an oath privately, when it is to further the ends of justice ? "

The officer's eyes were still keenly fixed on Alice Dalrymple's, and she cowered visibly beneath his gaze. He was puzzled by her evident terror. "Will you assure *me*, on your sacred word, that no person did enter the room ?" he repeated, in a low, firm tone ; which somehow carried to her the impression that he believed her to be trifling with them.

She looked at him ; gasped, and looked again ; and then she raised her handkerchief in her hand and wiped her ashy face.

" I think someone did come in," whispered the officer in her ear ; " try and recollect who it was." And Alice fell back in hysterics, and was taken from the room.

" Miss Dalrymple has been an invalid for

years; she is not strong like other people," remarked Lady Sarah. "I felt sure we should have a scene of some kind, and that is why I wished the investigation not to be gone into hurriedly."

"Don't you think there are good grounds for an investigation, sir?" testily asked Colonel Hope of the officer.

"I must confess I do think so, Colonel," was the reply.

"Of course: you hear, my lady. The difficulty is, how can we obtain the first clue to the mystery?"

"I do not suppose there will be an insuperable difficulty," observed Mr. Pullet. "I believe I have obtained one."

"You are a clever fellow, then," cried the Colonel, "if you have obtained it here. What is the clue?"

"Will Lady Sarah allow me to mention it—whatever it may be—without taking offence?" continued the officer, looking at her ladyship.

She bowed her head, wondering much.

"What's the good of standing upon cere-

mony ? " peevishly put in Colonel Hope.
" Her ladyship will be as glad as we shall be
to get back her bracelet; more glad, one
would think. A clue to the thief! Come!
who is it ? "

Mr. Pullet smiled. When men have been
as long in the police force as he had, they
give every word its due significance. " I
did not say a clue to the thief, Colonel: I
said a clue to the mystery."

" Where's the difference ?"

"Pardon me, it is perceptible. That the
bracelet is gone, is a palpable fact: but by
whose hands it went, is as yet a mystery."

" What do you suspect ? "

"I suspect," returned the officer, lowering
his voice, " that Miss Dalrymple knows how
it went."

There was a silence of surprise; on Lady
Sarah's part, of indignation.

" Is it possible that you suspect _her_ ? "
demanded Colonel Hope.

" No," said the officer, "I do not suspect
herself: she appears not to be a suspicious
person in any way : but I believe she knows

who the delinquent is, and that fear, or some other motive, keeps her silent. Is she on familiar terms with any of the servants?"

"But you cannot know what you are saying!" interrupted Lady Sarah. "Familiar with the servants! Miss Dalrymple is a gentlewoman; she has always moved in good society. Her family is little inferior to mine; and better—better than the Colonel's," concluded her ladyship, determined to speak out.

"Madam," said the officer, "you must be aware that in an investigation of this nature we are compelled to put questions which we do not expect to be answered in the affirmative. Colonel Hope will understand what I mean, when I say that we call them 'feelers.' I did not expect to hear that Miss Dalrymple had been on familiar terms with your servants (though it might have been); but that question, being disposed of, will lead me to another. I suspect that some one did enter the room and make free with the bracelet, and that Miss Dalrymple must have been cognizant of it. If a common thief, or an absolute stranger, she would have been the first to give the alarm : if not on too familiar terms with the servants, she would be as little likely to screen them. So we come to the question— who could it have been ? "

" May I inquire why you suspect this of Miss Dalrymple ? " coldly demanded Lady Sarah.

" Entirely from her manner; from the agitation she displays."

" Most young ladies, particularly in our class of life, would betray agitation at being brought face to face with a police-officer," urged Lady Sarah.

" My lady," he returned, " we are keen, experienced men ; and we should not be fit for the office we hold if we were not. We generally do find lady witnesses betray uneasiness when first exposed to our questions, but in a very short time, often in a few moments, it wears off, and they grow gradually easy. It was not so with Miss Dalrymple. Her agitation, excessive at first, increased visibly, and it ended as you saw. I did not think it the agitation of guilt, but I did think it that of conscious fear. And look at the related facts : that she laid the bracelets there, never left them, no one came in, and yet the most valuable one vanished. We have many extraordinary tales brought before us, but not quite so extraordinary as that."

The Colonel nodded approbation. Lady Sarah began to feel uncomfortable.

"I should like to know whether anyone called whilst you were at dinner," mused the officer. "Can I see the man who attends to the hall door ? "

"Thomas attends to that," said the Colonel, ringing the bell. "There is a side door, but that is only for the servants and tradespeople."

"I heard Thomas say that Sir George Danvers called while we were at dinner," observed Lady Sarah. "No one else. And Sir George did not go upstairs."

The detective smiled. "If he had gone, my lady, it would have made the case no clearer."

"No," laughed Lady Sarah, "poor old

Sir George would be puzzled what to do with a diamond bracelet."

"Will you tell me," said the officer, wheeling sharply round upon Thomas when he entered, "who it was that called here yesterday evening, while your master was at dinner? I do not mean Sir George Danvers; the other one."

Thomas visibly hesitated: and that was sufficient for the lynx-eyed officer. "Nobody called but Sir George, sir," he presently said.

The detective stood before the man, staring him full in the face with a look of amusement. "Think again, my man," quoth he. "Take your time. There was some one else."

The Colonel fell into an explosion: reproaching the unfortunate Thomas with having eaten his bread for five years in India, to turn upon the house and its master at last, and act the part of a deceitful, conniving wretch, and let in that swindler ——

"He is not a swindler, sir," interrupted Thomas.

"Oh no, not a swindler," roared the

Colonel; "he only steals diamond bracelets."

"No more than I steal 'em, sir," again
spoke Thomas. "He's not capable, sir. It
was Mr. Gerard."

The Colonel was struck speechless: his
rage vanished, and down he sat in a chair,
staring at Thomas. Lady Sarah coloured
with surprise.

"Now, my man," cried the officer, "why
could you not have said it was Mr. Gerard?"

"Because Mr. Gerard asked me not to say
he had been, sir; he is not friendly here,
just now; and I promised him I would not.
And I am sorry to have had to break my
word."

"Who is Mr. Gerard, pray?"

"He is my nephew," interposed the check-
mated Colonel. "Gerard Hope."

"But, as Thomas says, he is no swindler,"
remarked Lady Sarah: "he is not the thief.
You may go, Thomas."

"No, sir," stormed the Colonel; "fetch
Miss Dalrymple here first. I'll come to the
bottom of this. If he has done it, Lady

Sarah, I will bring him to trial; though he is Gerard Hope."

Alice came back, leaning on the arm of Lady Frances Chenevix; the latter having been dying with curiosity to come in before.

"So the mystery is out, ma'am," began the Colonel to Miss Dalrymple: "it appears this gentleman was right, and that somebody did come in. And that somebody was the rebellious Mr. Gerard Hope."

Alice was prepared for this, for Thomas had told her Mr. Gerard's visit was known; and she was not so agitated as before. It was the fear of its being found out, the having to conceal it, which had troubled her.

"It is not possible that Gerard can have taken the bracelet," said Lady Sarah.

"No, it is not possible," replied Alice. "And that is why I was unwilling to mention his having come up."

"What did he come for?" thundered the Colonel.

"It was not an intentional visit. I believe he only followed the impulse of the moment.

He saw me at the front window ; and Thomas, it appears, was standing at the door. He ran across, and came up."

"I think you might have said so, Alice," observed Lady Sarah, in a stiff tone.

"Knowing he had been forbidden the house, I did not wish to bring him under the Colonel's displeasure," was all the excuse Alice could offer. "It was not my place to tell of him."

"I presume he approached sufficiently near the bracelets to touch them, had he wished ?" observed the officer, who of course had now made up his mind upon the business—and upon the thief.

"Y—es," returned Alice, wishing she could have said No.

"Did you notice the bracelet there, after he was gone ? "

"I cannot say I did. I followed him from the room when he left, and then I went into the front room, so that I had no opportunity of observing the bracelets."

"The doubt is solved," was the mental comment of the detective officer.

The Colonel, hot and hasty, sent several servants various ways in search of Gerard Hope. He was speedily found, and brought; coming in with a smile on his frank, good-looking face.

"Take him into custody, officer," was the Colonel's impetuous command.

"Hands off, Mr. Officer—if you are an officer," cried Gerard, in the first shock of the surprise, as he glanced at the gentlemanly appearance of the other, who wore plain clothes. "You shall not touch me, unless you can show legal authority. This is a shameful trick. Colonel—excuse me for speaking plainly—as I owe nothing to you, I do not see that you have any right, or power, to bring about my arrest."

The group would have made a fine study: especially Gerard, his head thrown back in defiance, and looking angrily at everybody.

"Did you hear me?" cried the Colonel.

"I must do my duty," said the police-officer, approaching Gerard. "And for authority—you need not suppose I should act without it."

"Allow me to understand a little first," remarked Gerard, haughtily eluding the officer. "What is it for? What is the sum total?"

"Two hundred and fifty pounds," growled the Colonel. "But if you are thinking to compromise it in that way, young sir, you will find yourself mistaken."

"Oh, no fear," retorted Gerard; "I have not two hundred and fifty pence. Let me see: it must be Dobbs's. A hundred and sixty—how on earth do they slide the expenses up? I did it, sir, to oblige a friend."

"The deuce you did!" echoed the Colonel, who understood nothing of the speech except the last sentence. "I never saw a cooler villain in all my experience!"

"He was awfully hard up," went on Gerard, "as much so as I am now; and I did it. I don't deny having done such things on my own account, but from this particular one I did not benefit a shilling."

His calm assurance, and his words, struck them with consternation. You see, he and they were at cross purposes.

"Dobbs said he'd take care I should be put to no inconvenience—and this comes of it! That's trusting your friends. He vowed to me, this very week, that he had provided for the bill."

"He thinks it is only an affair of debt!" screamed Frances Chenevix. "Oh, Gerard! what a relief! We thought you were confessing."

"You are not arrested for debt, sir," explained the officer. "You are apprehended for—in short, it is a case of felony."

"Felony!" echoed Gerard Hope. "Oh, indeed! Could you not make it murder?" he added, with sarcasm.

"Off with him to Marlborough Street, officer," cried the exasperated Colonel; "I'll come with you and prefer the charge. He scoffs at it, does he?"

"Yes, that I do," answered Gerard. "Whatever pitfalls I may have walked into in the way of debt and carelessness, I have not gone in for felony."

"You are accused, sir," said the officer, "of stealing a diamond bracelet."

" Hey ! " uttered Gerard, a flash of in-
telligence rising to his face, as he glanced at
Alice. " I might have guessed it was the
bracelet affair, if I had had my recollection
about me."

"Oh, ho," triumphed the Colonel, in mocking jocularity. " So you expected it was the
bracelet, did you ? We shall have it all out
presently."

" I heard of the bracelet's disappearance,"
said Gerard. "I met Alice when she was
out this morning, and she told me it was
gone."

" Better make no admissions," whispered
the officer in his ear. " They may be used
against you."

" Whatever admissions I may make, you
are at liberty to use them," haughtily returned
Gerard. " Is it possible that you do suspect
me of taking the bracelet, uncle ?—or is this
a joke ? "

" Allow me to say a word," panted Alice,
stepping forward. " I—I—did not accuse
you, Mr. Hope ; I would not have mentioned
your name in connection with it, because I am

sure you are innocent; but when it was discovered that you had called, I could not deny that you were upstairs while the bracelets lay on the table."

"Of course I was. But the idea of my taking one is absurdly preposterous," went on Gerard. "Who accuses me?"

"I do," said Colonel Hope.

"Then I am very sorry it is not somebody else, sir, instead of you."

"Explain. Why?"

"Because they should get a kindly taste of my cane across their shoulders."

"Gerard," interrupted Lady Sarah, "do not treat it in that light way. If you did take the bracelet, say so, and you shall be forgiven. I am sure you must have been put to it terribly hard; only confess it, and the matter shall be hushed up."

"No, it shan't, my lady," cried the Colonel. "I will not have him encouraged—I mean, felony compounded."

"It shall," persisted Lady Sarah—"it shall indeed. The bracelet was mine, and I have a right to do as I please. Believe me,

Gerard, I will put up with the loss without a murmur : only confess, and let the worry be done with."

Gerard Hope looked at her : little trace of shame was there in his countenance. "Lady Sarah," he asked, in a deeply earnest tone, " can you indeed deem me capable of taking your bracelet ? "

" The bracelet was there, sir ; and it went ; and you can't deny it," cried the Colonel.

" The bracelet was there, sure enough," assented Gerard. "I held it in my hand for two or three minutes, and was talking to Alice about it. I told her I wished it was mine— and I said what I should do with it if it was."

"Oh, Mr. Hope, pray say no more," involuntarily interrupted Alice.

" What do you want to screen him for ? " impetuously broke forth the Colonel, turning upon Alice. "Let him say what he was going to say."

" I do not know why I should not say it," Gerard Hope answered, in his spirit of bravado, which he disdained to check. "I said I should pledge it."

"You'll send off to every pawnbroker's in the metropolis, before the night's over, Mr. Officer," cried the choking Colonel, breathless with rage. "This beats brass."

"But I did not take it any the more for having said that," put in Gerard, in a graver tone. "The remark might have been made by anyone, from a duke downwards, if reduced to his last shifts, as I am. I said *if* it were mine: I did not say I would steal it. Nor did I."

"I saw him put it down again," said Alice, in a calm, steady voice.

"Allow me to speak a word, Colonel," resumed Lady Sarah, interrupting what her husband was about to say. "Gerard—I cannot believe you guilty; but consider the circumstances. The bracelet was there: you acknowledge it: Alice left the apartment when you did, and went into the front room, and stayed there with the bracelets in view. Yet when I came up from dinner, it was gone."

The Colonel would speak. "So it lies between you and Miss Alice," he put in.

" Perhaps you would like us to believe she appropriated it."

" No," answered Gerard, with a flashing eye. "*She* cannot be doubted. I would rather take the guilt upon myself, than allow her to be suspected. Believe me, Lady Sarah, we are both innocent."

" The bracelet could not have gone without hands to take it, Gerard," replied Lady Sarah. " How else do you account for its disappearance ? "

" I believe there must be some misapprehension, some great mistake, in the affair altogether, Lady Sarah. It appears incomprehensible now, but it will be unravelled."

" Ay, and in double-quick time," wrathfully exclaimed the Colonel. " You must think you are talking to a pack of idiots, Master Gerard. Here the bracelet was spread temptingly out on a table ; you went into the room, being hard up for money, fingered it, wished for it, and both you and the bracelet disappeared. Sir "—turning sharply round to Mr. Pullet—" did a clearer case ever go before a jury ! "

Gerard Hope bit his lip. "Be more just, Colonel," said he. "Your own brother's son steal a bracelet!"

"And I am happy my brother is not alive to know it," rejoined the Colonel, in an obstinate tone. "Take him in hand, Mr. Officer: we'll go to Marlborough Street. I'll just change my coat, and ——"

"No, no, you will not," cried Lady Sarah, laying hold of the dressing-gown and the Colonel in it. "You shall not go; or Gerard, either. Whether he is guilty or not, it must not be brought against him publicly. He bears your name, Colonel, and so do I, and it would reflect disgrace on us all."

"Perhaps you are made of money, my lady. If so, you may put up with the loss of a two hundred and fifty guinea bracelet. *I* don't choose to do so."

"Then, Colonel, you will and you must. Sir," added Lady Sarah to the detective, "we are obliged to you for your attendance and advice, but it turns out to be a family affair, as you perceive, and we must decline to prosecute. Besides, Mr. Hope may not be guilty."

Alice rose, and stood before Colonel Hope. " Sir, if this charge were preferred against your nephew ; if it came to trial ; I think it would kill me. You know my unfortunate state of health ; the agitation, the excitement of appearing to give evidence would be—I—I cannot continue ; I cannot speak of it without terror. I *pray* you, for my sake, do not prosecute Mr. Gerard."

The Colonel was about to storm forth an answer, but her white face, her heaving throat, had some effect upon him. Perhaps also he was thinking of his dead brother. " He is so doggedly obstinate, you see, Miss Dalrymple ! If he would but confess, and tell where it is, perhaps I'd let him off."

Alice thought somebody else was obstinate. " I do not believe he has anything to confess," she deliberately said ; " I truly believe that he has not. He could not have taken it, unseen by me : and when we quitted the room, I feel sure the bracelet was left in it."

" It was," said Gerard. " When I left the room, I left the bracelet in it, so help me Heaven ! "

"And, now, I shall speak," put in Frances Chenevix. "Colonel, if you press the charge against Gerard, I will go before the magistrate, and proclaim myself the thief. I vow and protest I will; just to save him. And you and Sarah could not prosecute *me*, you know."

"*You* do well to stand up for him!" retorted the Colonel. "You would not be quite so ready to do it, my Lady Fanny, if you knew something I could tell you."

"Oh yes, I should," returned the young lady, with a vivid blush.

The Colonel, beset on all sides, had no choice but to submit; but he did so with an ill grace, and dashed out of the room with Mr. Pullet, as fiercely as though he had been charging an enemy at full tilt. "The sentimental apes these women make of themselves!" cried he, in his polite way, when he got Mr. Pullet in private. "Is it not a clear case of guilt!"

"In my private opinion, it certainly is," was the reply; "though he carries it off with a high hand. I suppose, Colonel, you still wish the bracelet to be searched for?"

" Search in and out, high and low; search everywhere. The rascal! to dare even to enter my house in secret!"

"May I be allowed to inquire, Colonel, whether the previous estrangement between you and your nephew had anything to do with money matters?"

"No," said the Colonel, turning more crusty at the thoughts called up. "I fixed upon a wife for him, and he wouldn't have her; so I turned him out of doors and stopped his allowance."

"Oh," was the only comment of Mr. Pullet.

So Gerard was allowed to go out of the house, a free man.

It was the following week, and Saturday night. Thomas was standing at Colonel Hope's door without his hat, a pastime he much favoured, chatting sociably with an acquaintance, when he perceived Gerard come tearing up the street. Thomas's friend backed against the rails and the spikes, and Thomas himself stood with the door in his hand, ready to touch his hair to Mr. Gerard, as he passed.

Instead of passing, however, Gerard cleared the steps at a bound, pulled Thomas with himself inside, shut the door, and double-locked it.

Thomas was surprised in all ways. Not only at Mr. Hope's coming in at all, for the Colonel had most solemnly interdicted it, but at the suddenness and strangeness of the action.

"Cleverly done," quoth Gerard, when he could get his breath. "I saw a shark after me, Thomas, and had to make a bolt for it. Your having been at the door saved me."

Thomas turned pale. "Mr. Gerard, you have locked it, and I'll put up the chain, if you order me, but I'm afeard it's going again the law to keep out them detectives by force of arms."

"What's the man's head running on now?" returned Gerard. "There are no detectives after me: it was only a seedy sheriff's officer. Psha, Thomas! there's no worse crime attaching to me than a slight suspicion of debt."

"I'm sure I trust not, sir: only master will have his own way."

" Is he at home ? "

" He is gone to the opera with my lady.
The young ladies are upstairs alone. Miss
Dalrymple has been ill, sir, ever since the
bother of the bracelet, and Lady Frances is
staying at home with her."

" I'll go up and see them. If the Colonel
and my lady are at the opera, we shall be
snug and safe."

"Oh, Mr. Gerard, had you better go up, do
you think ? " the man ventured to remark.
"If the Colonel should come to hear of it ——"

" How can he ? You are not going to tell
him, and I am sure the young ladies will not.
Besides, there's no help for it : I can't go out
again for hours yet. And, Thomas, if any
demon should knock and ask for me, I am
gone to—to—an evening party at Putney :
went out, you know, by the other door."

Thomas watched him run up the stairs, and
shook his head, thinking deeply. " One can't
help liking him, with it all : though where
could the bracelet have gone to, if he did not
take it ? "

The drawing-rooms were empty, and Gerard

made his way to a small room that Lady
Sarah called her boudoir. There they were:
Alice buried in the pillows of an invalid chair,
and Lady Frances careering about the room,
apparently practising some new mode of
waltzing. She did not see him: Gerard
danced up to her, took her hands and joined
in it.

"Oh!" she cried, with a little scream of
surprise, "you! Well, I have stayed at
home to some purpose. But how could you
think of venturing within these sacred and forbidden walls? Do you forget that the Colonel
threatens us with the terrors of the law, if we
suffer you to enter? You are a bold man,
Gerard."

"When the cat's away, the mice can play,"
said Gerard, treating them to a pas seul.

"Mr. Hope!" remonstrated Alice, lifting
her feeble voice. "How can you indulge in
these spirits, while things are so miserable?"

"Sighing and groaning won't make things
light," he answered, sitting down on a sofa
near to Alice. "Here's a seat for you, Fanny;
come along," he added, pulling Frances to his

side. "First and foremost, has anything come to light about that mysterious bracelet?"

"Not yet," sighed Alice. "But I have no rest: I am in hourly fear of it."

"*Fear!*" uttered Gerard, in astonishment.

Alice winced, and leaned her head upon her hand: she spoke in a low tone.

"You must understand what I mean. The affair has been productive of so much pain and annoyance to me, that I wish it could be ignored for ever."

"Though it left me under a cloud," said Gerard. "You must pardon me if I cannot agree with you. My constant hope is, that daylight may soon be let in upon it. I assure you I have specially mentioned it in my prayers."

"Pray don't!" reproved Alice.

"I'm sure I have cause to mention it, for it is sending me into exile. That, and other things."

"It is the guilty only who flee, not the innocent," said Frances. "You don't mean what you say, Gerard."

"Don't I! There's a certain boat advertised to steam from London Bridge wharf to-morrow, wind and weather permitting, and it will steam me with it. I am compelled to fly my country."

"Be serious, and say what you mean."

"Seriously, then, I am over head and ears in debt. You know my uncle stopped my allowance in the spring, and sent me—metaphorically speaking—to the dogs. It got wind; ill-news always does get wind; I had a few liabilities, and they have all come down upon me. But for this confounded bracelet affair, there's no doubt the Colonel would have settled them; rather than let the name of Hope be dubiously bandied by the public, he would have expended his ire in growls, and then gone and paid up. But that resource is over now; and I go to take up my abode in some renowned colony for desolate Home subjects, beyond the pale of British lock-ups. Boulogne, or Calais, or Dieppe, or Ostend; I don't know which of the four I shall stay in: and there I may be kept for years."

Neither of the young ladies answered immediately. They saw the facts were difficult, and that Gerard was only making light of it before them.

"How shall you live?" questioned Alice. "You must live there as well as here: you cannot starve."

"I shall just escape the starving. I am possessed of a trifle; enough to keep me on potatoes and salt. Upon my word it's little more. Perhaps I may get some writing to do for the newspapers? Don't you envy me my prospects?"

"When do you suppose you may return?" inquired Lady Frances. "I ask it seriously, Gerard."

"I know no more than you, Fanny. I have no expectations but from the Colonel. Should he never relent, I am caged there for good."

"And so you have ventured here to tell us this; and to bid us good-bye?"

"No; I never thought of venturing here," was the candid answer: "how could I tell that the Bashaw would be at the opera? A shark set on me in the street, and I had to run for my life. Thomas happened to be conveniently at the open door, and I rushed in, and saved myself."

"A shark!" exclaimed Alice, her inexperience taking the words literally—"a shark in the street!" Frances Chenevix laughed.

"One with sharp eyes and nimble feet, Alice, speeding after me with a polite invitation from one of the law lords. He is watching outside now."

"How shall you get away?" wondered Frances.

"If the Bashaw comes home before twelve, Thomas must dispose of me somewhere in the lower regions: Sunday is a free day for us, thank goodness. So please to make the most of me, both of you, for it is the last time you will have the privilege. By the way, Fanny, will you do me a favour? There used to be a little book of mine in the glass book-case in the library; my name in it, and a mottled cover: I wish you would go and find it for me."

Lady Frances left the room with alacrity. Gerard immediately bent over Alice, and his tone changed.

"I have sent her away on purpose. She'll be half an hour rummaging, for I have not seen the book there for ages. Alice, one word before we part. You must know that it was for your sake I refused the marriage proposed to me by my uncle : you will not let me go into banishment without a hope ; a promise of your love to lighten it."

"Oh, Gerard," she eagerly said, "I am so glad you have spoken : I almost think I must have spoken myself, if you had not. Just look at me ? "

"I am looking at you," he fondly answered.

"Then look at my hectic face ; my constantly tired limbs ; my sickly hands : do they not plainly tell you that the topics you would speak of must be barred topics to me ? "

"Why should they be ? You will get stronger."

"Never. There is no hope of it. Many years ago, when the illness first came upon me, the doctors said I might grow better with time, but the time has come, and come, and come, and——gone ; and it has only left me a more confirmed invalid. To an old age I cannot live ; most probably but a few years ; ask yourself, Gerard, if I am one who ought to marry, and leave behind a husband to regret me ; perhaps children. No, no."

"You are cruel, Alice."

"The cruelty would be, if I selfishly allowed you to talk of love to me ; or, still more selfishly, let you cherish hopes that I would marry. When you hinted at this the other evening, the evening that wretched bracelet was lost, I reproached myself with cowardice, in not answering more plainly than you had spoken. I should have told you, Gerard, as I tell you now, that nothing, no persuasion from even the dearest person on earth, shall ever induce me to marry."

"You dislike me. I see that."

"I did not say so," answered Alice, with a glowing cheek. "I think it very possible that—if I could allow myself ever to dwell on such things—I should like you very much ; perhaps better than I could like anyone."

"And why will you not ? " he persuasively uttered.

"Gerard, I have told you. I am too weak

and sickly to be other than I am. It would be a sin, in me, to indulge hopes of it: it would only be deceiving myself and you. No, Gerard, my love and hopes must lie elsewhere."

" Where ? " he eagerly asked.

Alice pointed upwards. " I am learning to look upon it as my home," she whispered, " and I must not suffer hindrances to obscure the way. It will be a better home than even your love, Gerard."

Gerard Hope smiled. " *Even* than my love : Alice, you like me more than you admit. Unsay your words, my dearest, and give me hope."

" Do not vex me," she resumed, in a pained tone ; " do not seek to turn me from my duty. I—I—though I scarcely like to speak of these sacred things, Gerard—*I have put my hand to the plough :* even you cannot turn me back."

He did not answer; he only played with the hand he held between both of his.

" Tell me one thing, Gerard : it will be safe. Was not the dispute about Frances Chenevix ? "

He contracted his brow; and nodded.

"And you could refuse her! You must learn to love her, for she would make you a good wife."

"Much chance there is now of my making a wife of anyone!"

"Oh, this will blow over in time: I feel it will. Meanwhile ———"

"Meanwhile you destroy every hopeful feeling I thought to take with me to cheer me in my exile," was his impatient interruption. "I love you alone, Alice; I have loved you for months, nay years, truly, fervently; and I know that you must have seen that I did."

"Love me still, Gerard," she softly answered, "but not with the love you would give to one of earth; the love you will give —I hope—to Frances Chenevix. Think of me as one rapidly going; soon to be gone."

"Oh, not yet!" he cried, in an imploring tone, as if it were to be as she willed.

"Not just yet: I hope to see you return from exile. Let us say farewell while we are alone."

She spoke the last sentence hurriedly, for footsteps were heard. Gerard snatched her to him, and laid his face upon hers.

"What cover did you say the book had?" demanded Frances Chenevix of Gerard, who was then leaning back on the sofa, apparently waiting for her. "A mottled? I cannot see one anything like it."

"No? I am sorry to have given you the trouble, Fanny. It has gone, perhaps, amongst the 'have-beens.'"

"Listen," said Alice, removing her hand from before her face, "I hear a carriage stopping. Can they have come home?"

Frances and Gerard flew into the next room, whence the street could be seen. A carriage had stopped, but not at their house. "It is too early for them, yet," said Gerard.

"I am sorry things go so cross just now with you, Gerard," whispered Lady Frances. "You will be very dull over there."

"Ay; fit to hang myself, if you knew all. And the bracelet may turn up, and Lady Sarah be sporting it on her arm again, and I never know that the cloud is off me. No

chance that any of you will be at the trouble
of writing to a fellow."

"I will," said Frances. "Whether the
bracelet turns up, or not, I will write to you
sometimes, if you like, Gerard, and give you
all the news."

"You are a good girl, Fanny," returned
he, in a brighter accent, "and I will send
you my address as soon as I possess one.
You are not to turn proud, mind, and be off
the bargain, if you find it to be in a fish-
market, au cinquième."

Frances laughed. "Take care of yourself,
Gerard."

He took leave of them, and got out by the
aid of Thomas, contriving to elude the shark.
And the next day the friendly steamer conveyed him into exile on other shores. The
prevalent opinion at Colonel Hope's was, that
he paid his expenses with the proceeds of the
diamond bracelet.

Perhaps it was not only the "bother of
the bracelet," as Thomas phrased it, that
was rendering Alice Dalrymple so miserable.
That, of course, was bad enough to bear,

from its very uncertainty. But she was in trouble about her sister. Selina's debts had become known to the world, and the embarrassment into which they had flung her husband. What with her seven thousand pounds (at least) of debts, and the liabilities cast on Oscar by the two London seasons, he owed a sum of ten thousand pounds.

How was he to pay it? He knew not. That he should be a crippled man for years and years, obliged to live in the nearest possible way, before the debts and their attendant costs, in the shape of interest and expenses, could be worked off, he knew. Selina knew it now, and had the grace to feel repentant. They had shut themselves up at Moat Grange, were "immured in it," Selina called it, every outlay of every kind being cut down.

All these things tried Alice; and would try her more as the days went on. There was no corner on earth to which she could turn for comfort.

In the silent watches of the night, in the broad glare of noonday, one question was ever tormenting her brain—which of the two

had got the bracelet ?   Impossible though it
seemed to suspect either of stealing it, emphatically though they both denied it, common sense told Alice Dalrymple that one of
them it must have been.

CHAPTER IV.

AN UNPLEASANT RUMOUR.

ONCE more a year has gone its round, bringing again to London all the stir and bustle of another season. It is a lovely afternoon towards the close of May, and there is some slight commotion in Chenevix House. Only the commotion of an unexpected arrival. Lady Mary Cleveland with her infant child and its nurse had come up from Netherleigh on a short visit. The infant, barely four weeks old yet, was a very small and fretful young gentleman, who had chosen to make his appearance in the world two good months before the world expected him.

Nobody was at home but Lady Grace. She ran down the stairs to welcome her sister.

"My dear Mary! I am so glad to see

you! We did not expect you until Monday.
You are doubly welcome."

" I thought it would make no difference—
my coming a few days earlier, and without
warning you," said Lady Mary, as she kissed
her elder sister. " I am not very strong,
Grace, and Mr. Forth has been anxious that
I should have a change. This morning was
so warm and fine, and I felt so languid, that
he said to me, ' Why not start to-day ? ' So
he and my husband packed me off, whether I
would or no. Where's mamma ? "

" Mamma is out somewhere. Gone to see
the pictures I think," added Grace, as Lady
Mary turned, of her own accord, into a small,
cosey sitting-room that used to belong to the
girls, and which they had nicknamed the
' Hut.' " Harriet is with her."

Lady Mary looked surprised. " Harriet !
Are the MacIvors here ? "

" Oh dear, yes ; staying with us. They
came up from Scotland on Monday."

" I am rather sorry I came, then. It may
be an inconvenience. And there won't be a
bit of quiet in the house."

" It will be no inconvenience at all, Mary—what are you thinking of ? You are to have your old room, and the baby the room next it. As to the house, it shall be as quiet as you please. I assure you it is wonderfully changed, in that respect, since all you girls were at home together."

" That time seems ages ago," remarked Lady Mary. " What light-headed, frivolous girls we were—and how life's cares change us ! Fancy our all marrying and leaving you behind ! "

" There's Frances, also."

" I forgot Frances. She is at Sarah's, I suppose, as usual. She will be marrying next, no doubt. *I* always thought she would be one of the first to marry, though she is the youngest except Adela. And then it will be your turn, Grace."

Grace slightly shook her head. " It will never be mine, Mary—as I believe. I have settled down into an old maid—and I feel like one. I would rather not marry now; at least, I think so. The time has gone by for it."

"What nonsense you talk! Why, you are only about three or four and thirty, Grace, though you are the eldest. A woman is not too old to marry, at that age."

"Well, I am not anxious to marry," replied Grace. "Papa and mamma should have one of us with them in their old age; and Frances will no doubt marry. It will, I know, be all as God pleases. Morning by morning as I get up, I put myself into His good care, and beseech Him to undertake for me—to use me as He will."

Lady Mary Cleveland smiled. This was all very right, of course—Grace had always had a religious corner in her heart.

"And now tell me all the news of Netherleigh," began Grace, when her sister had taken some refreshment, and the small mite of a baby was asleep, and they were back again in the "Hut," Mary lying on the sofa. "How is Aunt Margery?"

"You have had this room refurnished!" cried Mary, looking about her—at the bright carpet and chintz curtains.

"Yes, this spring. It was so very shabby."

" It is very pretty now. Aunt Margery ?—
oh, she is fairly well. Not too strong, I
fancy. I went to the Court yesterday and had
lunch with her. She is my baby's godmother."

" Is she ? The baby's christened, then ?"

" As if we should bring him away from
home if he were not ! You will laugh at his
old-fashioned name, Grace—Thomas."

" Thomas is a very good name. It is
your husband's."

" Yes—and not one of his first wife's
children bear it. So I thought it high time
this one should."

" Why did your husband not bring you up
to-day ? "

" Because he has two funerals this afternoon—people are sure to die at the wrong
time," added Lady Mary, quaintly. " And
the vicar of the next parish, who is always
ready to help him, is away this week."

" And the godfathers ? — who are they,
Mary ? "

" My husband is one of them ; he has
stood to all his children. The other is Oscar
Dalrymple ?"

"Oscar Dalrymple?" echoed Grace.

"Yes. He is not a general favourite, but Mr. Cleveland likes him. And he thinks he has behaved very well in this wretched business of Selina's. The one we should have preferred to have for godfather, we did not like to ask—if you can understand that apparent contradiction, Gracie?"

"And who was that?" asked Grace, looking up.

"Francis Grubb. He has been so very, very kind to us, and we like and respect him so greatly, above all other men on the face of the earth, that we quite longed to ask him to stand to the poor little waif. On the other hand, he is so wealthy and so generous, that my husband thought it might look like coveting more benefits. And so we fixed on Mr. Dalrymple."

Grace mused.

"I never use my beautiful pony-carriage but I feel grateful to Mr. Grubb," went on Lady Mary. "And look how good he has been in regard to Charles!"

A slight frown at the last word contracted

Grace's fair and open brow, as though the
name brought her some kind of discomfort.
It was smoothed away at once.

"Are the Dalrymples still at Moat Grange?"
she asked.

"Still there; living like hermits, in the
most inexpensive manner possible, with two
servants only—or three, I forget which.
Two maids, I think it is; and a man who
has to do the garden — as much as one
man can do of it—and feed the two pigs,
and milk the cow, and see to the cocks and
hens."

A smile crossed Grace's lips. "Does
Selina like that kind of life!"

"Selina *has* to like it; at any rate, to put
up with it, and she does it with a good
grace. It is she who has reduced Oscar to
poverty; the least she can do is to share in
his retirement and retrenchments without
murmuring. Oscar is trying to let Moat
Grange, but does not seem able to succeed.
His own little place, Knutford, was let for a
term of years when he came into Moat
Grange, so they cannot retire to that."

"It was very sad of Selina to act so," sighed Grace.

"It was unpardonable," corrected Lady Mary. "She knew how limited her husband's income was. Thoughtlessness runs in the Dalrymple family. Poor Mrs. Dalrymple wanted to give up the cottage and the income Oscar allows her, and go out into the world to shift for herself; but Oscar would not hear of it. We respect him for it. Close he may be, rather crabbed in temper; but he has a keen sense of honour. It is said his debts amount to ten thousand pounds."

"Ten thousand pounds!" almost screamed Grace.

"Quite that. Though indeed I should have said Selina's debts, rather than his. Mr. Grubb's sister, Mary Lynn, comes sometimes to Netherleigh, to spend a week with Mrs. Dalrymple — who was to have been Mary's mother-in-law, you know, had things gone straight with Robert. What a sweet girl she is!"

"I have always thought Mary Lynn that, since I knew her."

" Do you see Alice Dalrymple often ?" continued Lady Mary.

" Pretty often, save when the Hopes are in Gloucestershire. Alice looks very delicate."

" The Colonel is not reconciled to Gerard yet ? "

" No ; and not likely to be. Poor Gerard is somewhere abroad."

" And that mysterious bracelet of Sarah's —I conclude it has never come to light. Grace," added Lady Mary, dropping her voice ; "is it still thought that Gerard helped himself to it !"

Grace shook her head. " The Colonel thinks so. And as long as he does he will never forgive him, or take him back to favour."

" Well, I don't know that he could be expected to. Poor Gerard ! If he did do it, he must have been reduced to some pitiable strait. And my husband's boy, Charley—do you see much of him, Grace ?"

" Oh, we see him now and then," replied Grace, in a tone of constraint.

" Adela has quite taken him up, we find.

It is a relief to us, for we feared she might
not; might even, we thought, resent having
him in the house. How kind Mr. Grubb was
over that; how considerately thoughtful!"
continued Lady Mary. "None can know how
truly good he is?"

"You are right there," acquiesced Grace.
"But he does not always find his reward."

"How does Adela behave to him now?"
questioned Lady Mary, who had understood
the last remark to apply to her sister Adela;
and again she dropped her voice as she asked
it.

"Just as usual. There's no improvement
in her."

The previous summer, when the marriage
of Lady Mary Chenevix took place with Mr.
Cleveland, he, the Rector, came up the day
before it, and stayed at Mr. Grubb's by invitation, to be in readiness for the morrow's
ceremony. Mr. Grubb liked the Rector;
he had felt deeply sorry for him when he was
left a widower with so many children, and
was glad he was going to have a new help-
mate and they a second mother. That night,

as they sat talking together after dinner—
Adela being at her mother's, deep in all the
wedding paraphernalia—the Rector opened
his heart and his sorrows to Mr. Grubb:
what a care his children were to him, and
what he should do to place his many sons
out in life. Charles, the second, was chiefly
on his mind now. The eldest son, Harry,
was in the army, and getting on well, expected to get his company soon. Charles,
who was then twenty years of age, had been
intended for the Church, but he had never
taken to the idea kindly, and was now evinc-
ing a most unconquerable dislike to it. "I
cannot force him into it," said the Rector,
sadly, "I must find some other opening for
him. He must go out and begin to earn a
living somehow—I have too many of them
at home. I suppose"—he added, in a hesi-
tating tone of deprecation—"you could not
make room for him in Leadenhall Street?"
But Mr. Grubb told the Rector that he would
gladly make room for him; and, amid the
grateful thanks of the Rector, it was decided
upon, there and then, Mr. Grubb being most

liberal in his arrangements. "I must find him a lodging," said the Rector; "perhaps some family would take him and board him." "No, no; he had better come here," said Mr. Grubb; "provided Adela makes no objection. Strange lodgings are the ruin of many a young fellow—and will be of many more. London lodgings are no true home for young men; they take to go abroad at night out of sheer loneliness, get exposed to the temptations of this most dangerous city, teeming with its specious allurements, and fall helplessly into its evil ways. Your son, Mr. Cleveland, shall come here and be sheltered from the danger, if my wife will have him."

Lady Adela apathetically consented, when the proposal was made to her: the lad might come if he liked, she did not care, was all she answered. And so Charles Cleveland came: and his father believed and declared that no man had ever been so good and generous as Mr. Grubb.

A tall, slender, gentlemanly, dark-eyed, and very handsome and somewhat idle young fellow Mr. Charles Cleveland turned out to

be. He took well enough to his duties in the
counting-house, far better than he had taken
to Latin and Greek and theology; and Mr.
Grubb was as kind to him as could be; and
the more active partner, Mr. Howard, not too
severe.

But at the close of winter, when Charles
Cleveland had been some months located in
Grosvenor Square, Lady Adela began to show
herself very foolish. She struck up a flirtation with him. Whether it was done out of
sheer ennui at the prolonged cold weather, or
in very thoughtlessness, or by way of invent-
ing another source of vexation for her husband, Adela set up a strong flirtation with
Charles Cleveland, and the world was already
talking of it and laughing at it. The matter,
absurd though it was in itself, was vexing
Grace Chenevix, and her sister's mention
of Charley brought the vexation before
her.

"We heard something about Adela last
week," spoke Lady Mary, maintaining her
low tone, "not at all creditable to her: but
we hope it is not true."

Grace Chenevix felt her face flush. She assumed that her sister alluded to what was filling her thoughts, and she would have been glad to be spared speaking of it.

"It is but nonsense, Mary. It comes of sheer idle thoughtlessness on Adela's part, nothing more. Rely upon that."

"I am glad to hear you say so, Grace. But—do you ever go there with her?"

"Go where with her?"

"To Lady Sanely's."

The two sisters gazed at one another. They were at cross purposes.

"To Lady Sanely's?" exclaimed Grace in surprise. "I don't go there with Adela; I don't go there at all. Mamma has scarcely any acquaintance with Lady Sanely."

"Then how can you speak so confidently?" returned Mary Cleveland. "Adela may be quite deep in the mischief, for all you know."

"Mary, I do not understand you. You must explain what you mean."

"It is said," whispered Mary, glancing round at the walls, as if to reassure herself no one else was present, " that Adela has taken to gambling. That ——"

" To gambling ? " gasped Grace.

Lady Mary nodded. " It is said that gambling to a very dangerous extent is carried on at Lady Sanely's ; and that Adela has been drawn into the snare, and goes there nightly, and plays deeply. How do you think we heard this ? "

" Heaven knows," cried poor Grace, feeling a conviction that it might be true.

" From Harry ; my husband's eldest son. He has got his promotion at last, as perhaps you know, and is daily expecting orders to embark for India. He ran down last week to see us, and it was he who mentioned it. My husband told him to be careful ; that it could not be true. Harry maintained that it was true, and was, moreover, quite well known. He said he thought Lord Acorn was aware of it—but that Mr. Grubb was not."

" Papa *cannot* be aware of it," disputed Grace.

" Don't make too sure of it, Grace. Papa does a little in that line himself, you know ;

he may not look upon it in the dreadful light that you do, or that we people do in a rustic parsonage. Anyway, Harry says there's no mistake about Adela."

"Mr. Grubb ought to be warned—that he may save her."

"It is what my husband says—that Mr. Grubb ought to be told. I hope Adela has enough petty sins on her conscience!"

"This is the worst of all. She may ruin her husband, rich though he is."

"As poor Robert Dalrymple ruined himself. Scarcely that, however, in this case, Gracie. Mr. Grubb cannot be brought to ruin blindfold by his wife : and it strikes me he will take very good care, for her sake as well as his own, that she does not bring him to it. But he ought to be told without delay."

Grace Chenevix fell into one of the most unpleasant reveries she had ever experienced. Adela went often to Lady Sanely's ; she knew that. Another moment, and Lord Acorn came in.

"Papa," cried Lady Mary, after she had greeted her father, "we were talking of

Adela. A rumour reached us at Netherleigh that she was growing too fond of card-playing. It is carried on to a high extent at Lady Sanely's house, as we are led to believe, and that Adela is often there, and joining in it."

"Ay, they go in for tolerably high stakes at Lady Sanely's," replied the Earl, in his careless, not to say supercilious manner. " Very silly of Adela ! "

" It is true then, papa ! " gasped Grace.

" True enough," he remarked. " I dare-say, though, Adela can take care of her purse strings, and draw them in when necessary."

" How indifferent papa is ! " thought Grace, with a sigh.

She was anything but indifferent. She was thinking what it might be best to do ; how save Adela from further folly. After dinner, when the carriage came round to take her mother and Harriet to a small early gathering at old Lady Cust's, and Mary, tired with her day's journey, had retired for the night, Grace suddenly spoke.

" Mamma, I think, if you have no objec-tion, I will go with you in the carriage and

let it leave me at Adela's. I should like to
sit an hour with her."

"I have no objection," was the answer of
Lady Acorn, spoken rather tartly, as usual ;
for she lived in a chronic state of dissatisfac-
tion with her daughter Adela. "Go if you
like. And just give her a hint to mend her
manners, Grace, with regard to that boy."

"*That* is pure idle pastime," was the
mental comment of Grace Chenevix. "This
other may be worse."

CHAPTER V.

THEY stood together in the dusk of the evening, the tempter and the deceived. Really it is not too much so to designate them. She, one of the fairest of earth's fair daughters, leaned in a listless attitude against the window-frame, looking out on the square. Perhaps, listening : for a woman of misery, with three children round her, was singing her doleful ditty there, and gazing up at the noble mansion as if she hoped some poor mite might be dropped to her from its superfluity of wealth. The children were thin and haggard, with that sharp, pinching look of *age* in their faces so unsuited to childhood, and which never comes but from famine and long-continued wretchedness. The mother—she was little more than a girl—made a halt opposite the window : her eye had caught the

beautiful face enshrined there amidst the curtains, and she sang out louder and more
piteously than ever.

"Now I think that's real—no imposture—
none of those made-up cases that the Men-
dicity Society look up and expose."

The remark came from a young man, who
was likewise looking out, a very good-
looking young fellow of prepossessing countenance. There was an air of tenderness in his
manner as he spoke, implying tenderness of
heart for her who stood by him. And the
Lady Adela roused herself, and carelessly
asked, "What's real?" For her mind and
thoughts had been dwelling on invisible and
absent things, and the poverty and the singing
had remained to her as though it had not been.

"That poor wretch there, and those famished children. That one—the boy—looks
as if he had not tasted food for a week. See
how he fixes his eyes up here! I am sure
they are famished."

"Oh, Charles, don't talk so! Street beggars
ought not to be allowed to bring the sight of
their misery here. It makes one shiver.

They should confine themselves to the City, and such like low parts."

"What's that about the City," inquired Mr. Grubb, who had entered and caught the last words; while the young man, Charley Cleveland, moving listlessly towards a distant window, stealthily threw a shilling from it and then quitted the room.

"Street beggars," answered Adela. "I say they ought not to be allowed out of the City, exposing their rags and their wretchedness to us! It is too bad."

"The City is much obliged to you," said her husband in a marked manner, as if implying that he belonged to it. And the Lady Adela shrugged her shoulders in very French fashion, the gesture betraying contempt for the speaker and his words.

"Adela," he said, quietly drawing her to a sofa and sitting down beside her, "I have long wanted a few minutes' serious talk with you; and I have put it off from day to day, for the subject is full of pain to me, as it ought to be to you. Of shame, I had almost said."

She turned her lovely eyes upon him. He

could see the hard and defiant expression they
took, even in the twilight gloom.

"You may spare yourself the trouble of a
lecture—if that is what you intend. It will
do me no good."

"Whether it will do you good or not, you
must hear it. Your behaviour ———"

She interrupted him, humming a merry
tune.

"Adela, listen to me," he resumed; and
perhaps it was the first time she had heard
from him so peremptory a tone. "Your
behaviour is not what it ought to be; it is
not wise or seemly; and you must alter it."

"So you have told me ever since we were
married, all the four years and odd months,"
she said, with a half-playful, half-mocking
laugh.

"Of your behaviour to *me* I have told you
so repeatedly and uselessly that I have now
dropped the subject for ever. What I would
speak of is your behaviour to young Cleveland. The world is beginning to notice it;
and, Adela, what is objectionable in it *shall*
be discontinued."

" There is nothing objectionable—except in your imagination."

" There is : and you know it, Adela. You may treat me as you like; I cannot, unfortunately, alter that ; but I will guard *you* from being talked of. As to Cleveland ——"

" Charley," she broke in, turning her head to look for him ; " Charley, do you hear my husband ? He would like to——I thought Charley was here."

" Had he been here I should not have spoken," was Mr. Grubb's reply, signs of mortification on his refined and sensitive lips.

" Is your rôle going to be that of a jealous husband at last ? "

" No," he replied. " You have striven, with unnecessary endeavour, to deaden the love for you which once filled my heart ; if that love has not turned to gall and bitterness, it is not your fault. This is not a case for jealousy, Adela. You must know that. *I* jealous of a schoolboy ! "

" What is it a case of, then ? "

" Your fair reputation. That shall be cared for in the eyes of the world."

"There is no necessity for your caring for it," she retorted. "My reputation — and your honour—are perfectly safe in my own keeping. There lives not a man who could bring disgrace upon me. You are out of your senses, Mr. Grubb."

"That my honour is safe I do not doubt," he returned, drawing himself slightly up. "Forgive me if my words could have borne any other construction. I speak only of your reputation for folly—frivolity. The world is laughing at you : and I do not choose that it shall laugh."

A shade of annoyance flashed into her pretty face. "The world is nothing to me. It had better laugh at itself."

"Perfectly true. But I must take care it does not laugh at you. Your mother spoke to me to-day about Charles Cleveland. She called you a child, Adela ; and she said if I did not interfere and put a stop to it, she should."

"Let my mother mind her own affairs," was Adela's answer, full of resentment. "She can dictate to the two who are left to her, but not to the rest of us. When we married, we passed out of her control."

" Surely not. Your mother is always your mother."

" Pray where did you see her ? Has it come to secret meetings, in which my conduct is discussed ? "

"Nonsense, Adela ! Lady Acorn came to see me in Leadenhall Street, but upon other matters."

" And so you got up a nice little mare's nest between you ! That I was too fond of Charley Cleveland, and ought to be put in irons for it ! "

" That you were too *free* with him, Adela," corrected her husband. " That your manners with him, chiefly in this your own house, were losing that reserve which ought to temper them, though he is but a boy. It was she who said the world was laughing at you."

"And what did you say ? " asked Lady Adela, with an ill-concealed sneer.

" I said nothing," he replied, a sort of sadness in his tone. " I *could* have said that the subject had for some little time been to me a source of annoyance ; and I might have added that if I had refrained from remonstrance, it was because remonstrance from me to my wife had ever been worse than useless."

"That's true enough, sir. Then why attempt it now ?"

"For your own sake. And in years to come, when time shall have brought to you sense and feeling, you will thank me for being more careful of your fair fame than you seem inclined to be yourself. I do not wish to pursue the subject, Adela ; let the hint I have given you avail. Be more circumspect in your manners to young Cleveland. You know perfectly well that you are pursuing this senseless flirtation with him for one sole end—to vex me : you really care no more for him than for the wind that passes. But society, you see, not being behind the scenes, may be apt to attribute other motives to you. Change your tactics, *be true to yourself;* and then —— "

"And then ? Well ?"

"I shall not be called upon to interpose my authority. To do so would be against

my inclination and Charles Cleveland's interests."

" *Your* authority ! " she retorted, in a blaze
of scorn—for if there was one thing that put
out Lady Adela more than another it was to
be lectured: and she certainly did not like to
be told that the world was laughing at her.
" Have I ever altered my manners for any
authority you could bring to bear ?—do you
suppose that I shall alter them now ? Go and
preach to your people in the City, if you must
preach somewhere."

" Lady Grace Chenevix," interrupted the
groom of the chambers, throwing wide the
door.

" You are all in the dark ! " exclaimed
Grace. " I took the chance of finding you
at home, Adela. Mamma and Harriet are
gone to the Dowager Cust's."

" I am glad you came, Grace," said Mr.
Grubb, ringing for lights. " I wanted to look
in at the club for half an hour: you will stay
with Lady Adela."

" Grace," to his sister-in-law, " *Lady*
Adela " to his wife: what did that tell ?

Any way, it told that he had been provoked almost beyond bearing.

"Mary came up this afternoon, taking us by surprise," began Grace, as Mr. Grubb left the room, and the man retired after lighting the wax-lights. "She does not seem strong; and the baby is such a poor little —— "

"Pray are you a party to this conspiracy between my mother and him?" unceremoniously interposed Adela, with a fling of her hand towards the door by which her husband had disappeared, to indicate whom she meant by "him;" and the words were the first she had condescended to speak to her sister since her entrance.

"Conspiracy! I don't know of any," answered Grace, wondering what was coming.

"Had you been a few moments earlier, you would have found him holding forth about Charley Cleveland. And he said my mother went to him in the City to-day to put him up to it."

"Oh, if you mean about Charley Cleveland, I was going to speak to you of it myself. You are getting quite absurd about him,

Adela. Or he is about you. It was said at
Brookes's the other day that Charley Cleve-
land was losing his head for Lady Adela
Grubb."

Lady Adela laughed. "Who said it,
Gracie?"

"Oh, I don't know; a lot of them were
together. Captain Foster, and John Cust,
and Lord Deerhum, and Booby Charteries,
and others. It seems Charley was a little
overcome the previous evening. He and his
brother had been dining with the Guards,
very freely, and afterwards they went to—I
forget the place—somewhere that young men
do go to of an evening, and Charley finished
himself up with brandy and cigars; and then
he managed to hiccup out, that the only
angel living upon earth was Lady Adela
Grubb."

"And that's all!" she said, lightly—
"that Charley called me an angel! I told
him it was a mare's nest."

"No, it is not all," quickly answered Lady
Grace. "It might be all, if it were not for
your folly. I have seen Charley hold your

hand in his; I have seen him kiss it; I have seen him bend forward and whisper to you until his hair has all but touched yours. It is very bad, Adela."

"It is very amusing; it serves to pass away the time," laughed Adela. "And, pray, Grace, how came you to know so much of what they say and do at their clubs?"

"That's one of the annoying parts of it. Colonel Hope heard it; he was present. He went home, shocked and scared, to tell Sarah; and Sarah came yesterday morning and told mamma."

"Shocked and scared too? I should like to have seen Sarah's long face!"

"You should have seen mamma's. No wonder she went down to your husband. But that is not all yet, Adela. One of them, I think it was Lord Deerhum—whoever it was, had dined here a night or two before— told the others that you flirted with Charley desperately before your husband's eyes, and that while you showed favour to the one, you snubbed the other."

"And it's true," coolly avowed Adela.

" I like Charley Cleveland, and I *choose* to flirt with him. But if you strait-coated people think I have any wrong liking for him, you err woefully. Grace, all this is but idle talk. I shall *never* compromise myself by so much as a hazardous word, for Charley, or for anyone else. I have just told *him* so."

" Pleasant! the necessity for such an assertion to one's lord and master!"

" I never loved anybody in my life; and I'm sure I am not going to begin now. Not even Captain Stanley—though I did have a passing liking for him. Perhaps you will be surprised to hear, Grace, that there were odd moments in my life during the first year or two after my marriage, when I was nearer loving Francis Grubb than I had been of loving anyone—only that I had set out by steeling my heart against him."

Grace gazed at her sister wonderingly.

" But that's all past: and of love I feel none for any mortal man, and don't mean to feel it. But I like amusement—and I am amusing myself with Charley Cleveland."

"You have no right to do it, Adela. What is but sport to you, as it seems, may be death to him."

"That is his look-out," laughed Adela. "My private belief is, if you care to know it, that my husband was thinking as much of Charley as of me when he took upon himself to lecture me just now. Of the consequences to Charley's vulnerable and boyish heart; though he did put it upon me and on what the world might say."

"How grievously you must try your husband!" exclaimed Grace.

"He's used to it."

"You provoking woman! You'll never go to heaven, I should say, if only for your treatment of him. Adela, you made your vows before Heaven to love and honour him: how do you fulfil them?"

"I heard the other day you had turned Methodist; Bessy Cust came in and said it. I am sorry I contradicted it," cried the provoking Adela.

"You cannot set the world at defiance."

"I don't mean to. As to Charley dancing

attendance on me, or kissing my hand—what harm is there in it ? "

" That may be according to one's own notion of 'harm.' Even the most trifling approach to flirting is entirely unseemly in a married woman."

" Are you quite a competent judge—not being married yourself ? " rejoined Adela. " See here, Grace—if you never flirt worse with anyone than Charley flirts with me, you won't hurt."

" I am afraid he has learnt to *love* you, Adela."

" Then more silly, he, for his pains. Why, I am oceans of years older than Charley is. He ought to think of me as his grand-mother."

" *Can't* you be serious, child ? I want you to see the thing in its proper—or, rather, improper—light. When it comes to a man, other than your husband, kissing you, it is time ——"

" Who said Charley kissed me ? " retorted Adela, in a blaze of anger. " He has never done such a thing—never dared to attempt it.

I said he kissed my hand sometimes—and then it has generally had a glove upon it."

"Well, well, whatever the nonsense may be, you must give it up, Adela. There can be no objection on your part to do so, as you say you do not care for Charles Cleveland."

"Incorrect, Lady Grace. I do care for him; I enjoy his friendship amazingly. What I said was, that I did not love him. That would be too absurd."

"Call it flirtation, don't call it friendship," wrathfully retorted Grace. "And he must be as devoid of brains as a calf, to attach himself to you, if he has done it. I hope nothing of this will reach the ears of Mary or of his father. They would not believe him capable of such folly. From this hour, Adela, you must give it up."

"Just what Mr. Grubb has been good enough to tell me; but 'must' is a word I do not understand," lightly rejoined Adela. "Neither you nor he will make me break off my flirtation with Charles Cleveland. I shall go into it all the more to spite you."

" If I were Francis Grubb I should beat you, Adela."

"If!" laughingly echoed Lady Adela. " If you were Francis Grubb, you would do as he does. Why, Gracie, girl, he loves me passionately still, for all his assumed indifference. Do you think there are never moments when he betrays it ? He is jealous of Charley ; that's what he is, in spite of his dignified denial—and oh, the fun it is to me to have made him so ! "

" Adela," said Grace, sadly, " does it never occur to you that this behaviour may tire your husband out ?—that his love and his patience may give way at last ? "

" I wish they would ! " cried the provoking girl, little seeing or caring, in her reckless humour, what the wish might imply. " I wish he would go his way and let me go mine, and give me hundreds of thousands a year for my own share. He should have the dull rooms in the house and I the bright ones, and we would only meet at dinner on state occasions, when the world and his wife came to us."

Lady Grace felt downright angry. She wondered whether Adela spoke in her heart's true sincerity.

"There's no fear of it, Gracie : don't look at me like that. My husband would no more part company with me, whatsoever I might do, than he would part with his soul. He loves me too well."

"It is a positive disgrace to have one's married sister's name coupled with a flirtation," grumbled Grace : for the Lady Acorn, whatever might be her failings as to tongue and temper, had brought her daughters up in the purest and best of notions. "That reverend man, Dr. Short—I cannot think how it came to *his* ears—hinted at it to-day in talking with mamma when they met at the picture galleries. He ——"

"There it is ! " shouted Adela, in glee; "the murder's out ! So it is you who have been putting mamma up to complain to Mr. Grubb ! You are setting your cap at that sanctimonious Dr. Short, and you fear he won't see it if you have got a naughty sister given to flirting. Oh, Gracie ! "

" You are wrong ; you know you are wrong. How frivolous you are, Adela ! Dr. Short is going to be married to Miss Greatlands."

" Well, there's something of the sort in the wind, I know. If it's not the Reverend Dr. Short, it's the Reverend Dr. Long ; so don't shake your head at me, Gracie."

Dancing across the room, Adela rang the bell. " My carriage," she said to the servant.

" It has been waiting some time, my lady."

" Where are you going ? " asked Grace, surprised.

" To Lady Sanely's."

" To Lady Sanely's," echoed the elder sister. Then, after a pause, " Your husband did not know you were going there ? "

" Do you suppose I tell him of my engagements ? What next, I wonder ? "

" Oh, Adela ! " uttered Grace, rising from her seat—and there was a piercing sound of grief in her tone, deeper than any which had characterised it throughout the interview —" do not say you are going *there !* Another rumour is rife about you ; worse than that half-nonsensical one about Charles Cleveland; one likely to have a far graver effect on your welfare and happiness."

"I—I do not understand," repeated Adela; but her tone, in spite of its display of haughtiness, betrayed that she did understand, and it struck terror to the heart of her sister. "I think you are all beside yourselves to-day!"

Grace, greatly agitated, clasped the other's arm as she was turning away. "It is said, Adela—I have heard it, and papa has confirmed it—it is rumoured that you have become addicted to a—a—dangerous vice. Oh, forgive me, Adela! Is it so? You shall not go until you have answered me."

The rich colour in Lady Adela's cheeks had faded to paleness; her eyes drooped; she could not look her sister in the face. From this, her manner of receiving the accusation, it might be seen how much more real was this trouble, than the half-nonsensical one, as Grace had called it, connected with Charles Cleveland.

"Vice!" she vaguely repeated.

"That of gaming," spoke Grace, her own

voice unsteady in its deep emotion. "That you play deeply, night by night, at Lady Sanely's."

"What strong words you use!" gasped Adela, resentfully. "Vice! Just because I may take a hand at cards now and then!"

"Oh, my poor sister, my dear sister, you do not know what it may lead to!" pleaded Grace. "You shall not go forth to Lady Sanely's this night—do not! do not! Break through this dreadful chain at once—before it be too late."

Angry at hearing this amusement of hers had become known at home, vexed and embarrassed at being pressed, almost by force, to stay away from its fascinations, Adela flung her sister's arm from her and moved forward with an impatient gesture of passion. They were near a table, and her own hand, or that of Grace, neither well knew which, caught in a beautiful inkstand, and turned it over. The ink was scattered on the light carpet : an ugly, dark blotch.

What cared Adela ? If the costly carpet was spoiled, *his* money might purchase another.

She moved on to her dressing-room, caused her maid, waiting there, to envelop her in her evening mantle, and then swept down to her carriage.

That Lady Adela did not care for Charles Cleveland was perfectly true. She would have laughed at the very idea ; she regarded him but as a pleasant-mannered boy : nevertheless, partly to while away the time, which sometimes hung heavily on her hands, partly because she hoped it would vex her husband, whom she but lived to annoy, she had plunged into the flirtation.

It was something more on Charley's part. For, while Adela cared not for him, beyond the passing amusement of the moment, would not have given to him a regretful thought had he suddenly been removed from her sight for ever, he had grown to love her to idolatry. It is a strong expression, but in this case justifiable. Almost as the sun is to the world, bringing to it light and heat, life to flowers, perfection to the corn, so had Lady Adela become to him. In her presence he could alone be said to live ; his heart then was at rest, feeding on its own fulness of happiness, and there he could thankfully have lived and died, and never asked for change: when obliged to be absent from her, a miserable void was his, a feverish yearning for the hour that should bring him to her again. Surely this was most reprehensible on his part— to have become attached, in this senseless manner, to a married woman! Reprehensible? Hear what one says of another love; he who knew so much about love himself—Lord Byron:

"Why did she love him? Curious fool, be still :
Is human love the growth of human will?"

Could the fault have lain with Lady Adela? Most undoubtedly. She, not casting a thought to the effect it might have upon his heart, and secure in her own supreme indifference, purposely threw out the bait of her beauty and her manifold attractions, and so led him on to love—a love as true and impassioned as was ever felt by man. What did he promise himself by it?—what did he think could come of it? Nothing. He was not capable of cherish-

ing towards her a dishonourable thought, he
had never addressed to her a disloyal word.
It was not in the nature of Charles Cleveland
to do anything of the kind; he was single-
minded, single-hearted, chivalrously honourable. He thought of her as being all that
was good and beautiful: to him she seemed
to be without fault, sweet and pure as an
angel. To conceal his deep love for her was
beyond his power; eye, tone, manner, tacitly
and unconsciously betrayed it. And Lady
Adela, to give her her due, did not encourage
him to more.

And so, while poor Charley was living on
in his fool's paradise, wishing for nothing,
looking for nothing, beyond the exquisite
sense of bliss her daily presence brought him,
supremely content could he have lived on in it
for ever, Lady Adela already found the affair
was growing rather monotonous. The chances
were that had her husband and Grace not
spoken to her, she would very speedily have
thrown off Charley and his allegiance. Adela
had no special pursuit whence to draw daily
satisfaction. No home (the French would

better express it by the word ménage) to keep up and contrive for; the hand of wealth was at work, and all was provided for her to satiety; she had no children to train and love; she had no husband whom it was a delight to her to yield to, to please and cherish : worse than all, she had (let us say *as yet*) no sense of responsibility to a higher Being, for time and talents wasted.

A woman cannot be truly happy (or a man either) unless she possesses some aim in life, some daily source of occupation, be it work or be it pleasure, to contrive, and act, and live for. Without it she becomes a vapid, weary, discontented being, full of vague longings for she knows not what. One of two results is pretty sure to follow—mischief or misery. Lady Adela was too young and pretty to be miserable, therefore she turned to mischief.

Chance brought her an introduction to the Countess of Sanely, with whom the Chenevix family had no previous acquaintance, and who had a reputation for loving high card-playing and for encouraging it at her house : she and Adela grew intimate, and Adela was drawn into the disastrous pursuit. At first she liked it well enough; it was fascinating, it was new: and now, when perhaps she was beginning to be a little afraid and would fain have retreated, she did not see her way clear to do so: for she owed money that she could not pay.

Lady Grace Chenevix, unceremoniously left alone in her sister's drawing-room, rang the bell. It was to tell them to attend to the ink. The carriage was not coming for her till eleven o'clock, and it was now but half-past ten. Hers were not very pleasant thoughts with which to get through the solitary half-hour. Mr. Grubb came in, and inquired for his wife. Grace said she had gone out.

"What, and left you alone! Where's she gone to?"

"To Lady Sanely's."

"Who are these Sanelys, Grace?" he inquired as he sat down. "Adela passes four or five nights a week there. The other evening I took up my hat to accompany her, and she would not have it. What kind of people are they?"

" Four or five nights a week," mechanically repeated Grace, passing over his question. " And at what time does she get home ? "

" At all hours. Sometimes very late."

Grace sat communing with herself. Should she impart this matter of uneasiness to Mr. Grubb, or should she be silent, and let things take their chance ? Which course would be more conducive to the interests of Adela ? for she was indeed most anxious for her. She looked up at him, at his noble countenance, betraying commanding sense and intellect— surely to impart the truth to such a man was to make a confidant of one able to do for her sister all that could be done. Mr. Cleveland and Mary both said he ought to hear it without delay. And Grace's resolution was taken.

" Mr. Grubb," she said, her voice somewhat unsteady, " Adela is your wife and my sister ; we have both, therefore, her true welfare at heart. I have been deliberating whether I should speak to you upon a subject which—which—gives me uneasiness, and I believe I ought to do so."

"Stay, Grace," he interrupted. "If it is
—about—Cleveland, I would rather not enter
upon it. Lady Acorn spoke to me to-day,
and I have given a hint to Adela."

"Oh, no, it is not that. She goes on in
a silly way with him, but there's no harm
in it, only thoughtlessness. I am *sure* of
it."

He nodded his head, in acquiescence, and
began pacing the room.

"It is of her intimacy with Lady Sanely
that I would speak; these frequent visits
there. Do you know what they say?"

"No," he replied, assuming great indifference, his thoughts apparently directed to
placing his feet on one particular portion of
the pattern of the carpet, and to nothing else.

"They say—they do say"—Grace faltered, hesitated: she hated to do this, and
the question flashed across her, could she
avoid it?

"Say what?" said Mr. Grubb carelessly.

"That play to an incredible extent is
carried on there. And that Adela has been
induced to join in it."

His assumed indifference was forgotten now, and the carpet might have been patternless for all he knew of it. He had stopped right under the chandelier, its flood of light illumining his countenance as he looked long and hard at Grace, as one in a maze.

Much that had been inexplicable in his wife's conduct for some little time past was rendered clear now. Her feverish restlessness on the evenings she was going to Lady Sanely's ; her coming home at all hours, jaded, sick, out of spirits, yet unable to sleep ; her extraordinary demands for money, latterly to an extent which had puzzled and almost terrified him. But he had never yet refused it to her.

"It must be put a stop to somehow," said Grace.

"It must," he answered, resuming his walk, and drawing a deep breath. "What's all this wet on the carpet ?"

"An accident this evening. Some ink was thrown down. My fault, I believe. At any cost, any sacrifice," continued Lady Grace. "If the habit should get hold of

Adela, there is nothing but unhappiness before her—perhaps ruin."

" Any cost, any sacrifice, that I can make, shall be made," repeated Mr. Grubb. " But Adela will listen to no remonstrance from me. You know that, Grace."

" You must—stop the supplies," suggested Grace, dropping her voice to a confidential whisper. " Has she had much of late ? "

" Yes."

" More than her allowance ? Perhaps not, as that is so liberal."

" Her allowance ! " half laughed her husband, not a happy laugh. " It has been, to what she has drawn of me, as a silver coin in a purse of gold."

Grace clasped her hands. " And you let her have it ! Did you suspect nothing ? "

" Not of this nature. I suspected that she might be buying costly things—after the reckless fashion of Selina Dalrymple. Or else that—forgive me, Grace, I would rather not say more."

" Nay," said Grace, rising to put her hand on his arm and meeting his earnest glance, "let there be entire confidence between us; keep nothing back."

"Well, Grace, I fancied she might be lending it to your mother."

"No, no; my mother has not borrowed from her lately. Oh, how can we save her! This is an insinuating vice that gains upon its votaries, they say, like the eating of opium."

"Your carriage, my lady," interrupted a servant, entering the room. And Grace caught up her mantle.

"Must you go, Grace? It is scarcely eleven."

"Yes. If mamma does not have the carriage to the minute, she won't cease scolding for days, and it must take me home first. Dear Mr. Grubb, turn this over in your mind," she whispered, "and see what you can do. Use your influence with her, and be firm."

"My influence, did you say?" And there was a touch of sarcasm in his tone, mingled with a grief painful to hear. "What has my influence with her ever been, Grace!"

"I know, I know," she cried, wringing his

hand, and turning from him towards the stairs, that he might not see the tears gathering in her eyes. Tears of sympathy with his wrongs, and partly, perhaps, of regret: for she was thinking of that curious misapprehension, years ago, when she had been led to believe that it was herself who was his chosen bride. "*I* would not have treated him so," her heart murmured; "I would have made his life a happy one, as he deserves it should be."

He gained upon her fast steps; and, drawing her arm within his, led her downstairs, and placed her in the carriage.

"Dear Mr. Grubb," she whispered, as he clasped her hands, "do not let what I have been obliged to say render you harsh with poor Adela. Different days may be in store for you both; she may yet be the mother of your children, when happiness in each other would surely follow. Do not be unkind to her."

"Unkind to Adela! No, Grace. Separation, rather than unkindness."

"Separation!" gasped Grace, the ominous word affrighting her.

"I have thought sometimes that it may come to it. A man cannot patiently endure contumely for ever, Grace."

He withdrew his hand from hers, and turned back into his desolate home. Grace sank back in the carriage, with a mental prayer.

"God keep him! God comfort him; and help him to bear!"

CHAPTER VI.

IT was two o'clock when Lady Adela returned home. She ran lightly upstairs and into the drawing-room, throwing off her mantle as she came in. A tray of refreshments stood on a side-table.

Mr. Grubb rose from his chair. "It is very late, Adela."

"Late! Not at all. I wish to *goodness* you'd not sit up for me!"

She went to the table and stood looking at the decanters, as if deliberating what she should take, murmuring something about being "frightfully thirsty."

"What shall I give you?" he asked.

"Nothing," was the ungracious answer, most ungraciously spoken. And she poured out a tumbler of weak sherry-and-water, and drank it; a second, and drank that also.

Then, without taking any notice of him, she went up to her chamber. Anything more pointedly, stingingly contemptuous than her behaviour to her husband now, and for some time past, has never been exhibited by mortal woman.

Mr. Grubb rang for the man to put out the wax-lights, and went up in his turn. There was no sleep for him that night, whatever there might have been for her. He knew not how to act, how to arrest this new pursuit of hers; he scarcely knew even how to open the matter to her. She appeared to be asleep when he rose in the morning and passed into his dressing-room. She herself soon afforded him the opportunity.

He was seated at his solitary breakfast, a meal his wife rarely condescended to take with him, when her maid entered, bringing a message from her lady—that she wished to see him before he left for the City. Master Charley Cleveland, usually his breakfast companion, had not made his appearance at home since the previous night.

"Is your lady up, Davvy?"

"Oh dear yes, sir, and at breakfast in her dressing-room."

He went up to it. How very lovely she looked, sitting there at her coffee, in her embroidered white dress and pink ribbons, and the delicate lace cap shading her sweet features. She had risen thus early to get money from him; he knew that, before she asked for it.

"You wished to see me, Lady Adela."

"I want some money," she said, in a light, flippant kind of tone, as if it were the sole purpose of Mr. Grubb's existence to supply her demands for it.

"Impossible," he rejoined. "You had two hundred pounds from me the day before yesterday."

"I must have two hundred more this morning. I want it."

"What is it that you are doing with all this money? It has much puzzled me."

"Oh—making a purse for myself," she answered, saucily.

"You can trust me to do that for you. I cannot continue to supply you, Adela."

"But I must have it," she retorted, raising her voice, and speaking as though he were the very dirt under her feet. "I will have it."

"No," he replied calmly, but with firm resolution in his tone. "I shall give you no more until your allowance is due."

She looked up, quite a furious expression on her lovely face. "Not give it me! Why, what do you suppose I married you for?"

"Adela!" came his reproof, almost whispered.

"I would not have taken you but for your money; you know that. They promised me at home that I should have unlimited command of it; and I will."

"You have had unlimited command," he observed, and there was no irritation suffered to appear in his tone, whatever may have been his inward pain. "It is for your own sake I must discontinue to supply it."

"You are intelligible!" was her scornful rejoinder: for, in good truth, this refusal was making havoc of her temper.

"All that you can need in every way shall be yours, Adela. Purchase what you like, order what you like; I will pay the bills without a murmur. *But I will not give you money to waste, as you have latterly wasted it, at Lady Sanely's.*"

She rose from her seat, pale with anger. "First Charles Cleveland, then Lady Sanely: what else am I to be lectured upon? How dare you presume to interfere with my pursuits?"

"I should ill be fulfilling my duty to you, or my love either, Adela, what is left of it, if I did not interfere."

"I will not listen, Mr. Grubb: if you attempt to preach to me, as you did last night, I will run away. Sit down and write me a cheque for the money."

"There is no necessity for me to repeat my refusal, Adela. Until I have reason to believe that this new liking for PLAY has left you, you should draw my blood from me, sooner than money to pursue it. But remember," he impressively added, "that I say this in all kindness."

She looked at him, her delicate throat working, her breath growing short with passion.

" Will you give me the cheque ? "

" I will not. Anything more, Adela, for I am late ? "

There was no answer in words, but she suddenly raised the cup, which chanced to be in her hand and was half full of coffee, and flung it at him. It struck him on the chin, the coffee falling upon his clothes.

It was a moment of embarrassment for them both. He looked steadfastly at her, with a calm, despairing sorrow, and then quitted the room. While Lady Adela, her senses returning, sank back in her chair ; and in the reaction of her inexcusable passion, sobbed aloud.

It was quite a violent fit of sobbing : and she smothered her head up that he should not hear. She did feel ashamed of herself, felt even a little honest shame at her general treatment of him. As her sobs subsided, she heard him in his dressing-room, changing his things, and she wished she had not done it. But she *must* have the money ; that, and more ; and without it, she should be in a frightful dilemma, and might have her name posted up as a card-playing defaulter in the drawing-rooms of society.   So she determined to have another battle for it with her husband, and she dried the tears on her fair young face, and opened his dressing-room door quite humbly, so to say, and went into it.

It was empty.   Mr. Grubb's movements had been rapid, and he was already gone. He had put out of sight the stained things taken off, removed all traces of them.   Was she not sensible even of this ?   Did she not know that he was thus cautious for her own sake—that no scandal might be given to the tongues of the servants ?   Not she.   With his disappearance, and the consequent failure of her hope, all her resentment was returning. Her foot kicked against something on the floor, and she stooped to pick it up.   It was her husband's cheque-book, which he must have unconsciously dropped when transferring things from one pocket to another.

Was a demon just then at Lady Adela's side ?—what else could have impelled her ?— what else whispered to her of a way to supply the money she wanted ?   Once only a momentary hesitation crossed her; but she drove it away, and carried the cheques to her writing-table, and *used one of them.*

She drew it for five hundred pounds, a heavy sum, and she boldly signed it "Grubb and Howard." For it happened to be the cheque-book of the firm, not of her husband's private account. She was clever at drawing, clever at imitating styles of writing—not that she had ever turned her talent to its present use, or thought so to turn it—and the signature, when finished, looked very like her husband's own. Then she carried back the cheque-book, and laid it on the floor where she found it.

Some time after all this was accomplished, she was passing downstairs, deliberating upon whether she could dare to go to the bank herself to get the cheque cashed, when Charles Cleveland came in, and bounded up the stairs.

"Where did Mr. Grubb breakfast this morning?" he inquired, apparently in a desperate hurry, as they shook hands, and turned into one of the sitting-rooms, Charley devouring her with his eyes all the time. Little blame to him, either, for she was looking most lovely : the excitement, arising from what she had done, glowing in her cheeks like a sweet blush rose.

"What a question! He breakfasted at home."

"Yes, yes, dear Lady Adela. I meant in which room." For Mr. Grubb sometimes breakfasted in the regular breakfast-room, and sometimes in his library.

"I really don't know, and don't care," returned Adela, connecting the question somehow, in her own mind, with the present of coffee he had received. "His breakfasting is a matter of indifference to me. And pray, Mr. Charley, where did *you* breakfast this morning?—and what became of you last night? Have you been making a night of it with the owls and the bats?"

"I went to my brother's. Harry had some fellows with him, and we, as you express it, dear Lady Adela, made a night of it. That is, we broke up so late that I would not disturb your house by returning here : Harry gave me a sofa, and I went direct from him to Leadenhall Street this morning."

"And what have you come back for?"

"For Mr. Grubb's cheque-book. He has missed it, and thinks he must have left it on the breakfast-table."

"Charley," she said, "I was just wanting you. *Will* you do me a favour?"

"I will do everything you wish," he answered, his tones literally trembling with tenderness.

"I want you to go to the bank in Lombard Street, and get me a cheque cashed. Mr. Grubb gave it me this morning, and I am in a hurry for the money, for I expect people here every minute with some accounts. It is not crossed. Take a cab, and go at once."

"I will. I can leave the cheque book in Leadenhall Street first."

"No, you must not wait to find the cheque-book. I will look for it while you are gone. You will not be many minutes, I am sure, and I tell you I am all impatience."

Charley Cleveland hesitated. "I scarcely know what to say," he replied, dubiously, to this. "Mr. Grubb is waiting for the cheque-book. This is Saturday, you know."

" What if it is ? "

" We are always so busy on Saturdays."

" Very well, Charles," she returned, in a hurt, resentful tone. " If you like Mr. Grubb better than you do me, you will oblige him first. You would be there and back in no time."

" Dearest Lady Adela ! Like Mr. Grubb better than —— Well, I will do it, though I daresay I shall get into a row. Have the cheque-book ready, that I may not lose a moment when I get back." And Adela nodded assent.

" A confounded row, too," he muttered to himself, as he tore down the stairs, and into the cab ; " but I will go through a thunder-cloud full of rows for *her*." Charley gave a concise word to the driver, and away dashed the cab towards Lombard Street, at a pace which terrified the road generally, and greatly astonished the apple-stalls.

He was back in an incredibly short space of time, and paid the notes over to her. " Have you found the cheque-book ? " he asked then.

" I declare I never thought about it," was Lady Adela's reply. " But he breakfasted in the library, I hear. Perhaps you will find it there."

He rushed into the library. And there, on the table, was the missing cheque-book. Oh, wary Lady Adela!

She followed him into the room. "Charley," she whispered, " don't say you have been out for me—no need to say you have seen me. The fact is, that staid husband of mine got a grumbling fit upon him last night, and accused me of talking and laughing too much with the world in general and Mr. Charles Cleveland in particular. If they find fault with you for loitering, say you were detained on some matter of your own."

He nodded in the affirmative. But a red vermilion was stealing over his face, dyeing it to the very roots of his hair, and his heart's pulses were rising high. For surely in that last speech she meant to imply that she *loved* him. And Master Charles felt his brain turn round as it had never turned before, and he bent that flushed face down upon her hand,

and left on it an impassioned, though very respectful kiss, by way of adieu.

"What a young goose he is!" thought Adela.

Very ill at ease, that day, was the Lady Adela. Reckless though she might be as to her husband's good opinion, implicitly secure though she felt that he would hush up the matter and shield her from consequences, she could not help being dissatisfied with what she had done. Suppose *exposure* came?— she would not like *that*. She had written Mr. Howard's name, as well as her husband's! She lost herself in a reverie, her mind running from one ugly point to another. Try as she would, she could not drive the thoughts away, and by the afternoon she had become seriously uneasy. Was such a case ever known as that of a wife being brought to trial for —— "Whatever possesses me to dwell upon such things?" she mentally queried, starting up in anger with herself. "Rather order the carriage and go and pay my last night's losses."

From Lady Sanely's she went to her mother's, intending to stay and dine there.

Somehow she was already beginning to shrink from meeting her husband's face. However, she found they were all engaged to dine at Colonel Hope's, including her sister Mary. So Adela had to return home : but she took care not to do it until close upon the dinner hour.

Mr. Grubb and Charles Cleveland were both at table. Neither of them alluded to the unpleasant topic uppermost in her mind, so she concluded that as yet nothing had come out. Mr. Grubb was very silent—the result no doubt of the coffee in the morning.

" I am going to Netherleigh to-morrow morning, sir," observed Charles ; " shall get there in time for church. My father has written to ask me. Could you allow me to remain for Monday also ? Harry [means to run down that day, to say good-bye."

" Monday ? " considered Mr. Grubb. " Yes, I suppose you can. There's nothing particular that you will be required for on Monday, that I know of. You may stay."

" Thank you, sir."

" When does your brother leave ? "

" I think on Tuesday morning."

Accordingly, on the following morning, Sunday, Charley left the house to go to Netherleigh. Mr. Grubb went to church, as usual; Adela made an excuse—said her head ached. When he returned home at one o'clock, he found she had gone to her mother's; and, without saying to him with your leave, or by your leave, without, in fact, giving him any intimation whatever, she remained at Chenevix House for the rest of the day.

On the Monday, Mr. Grubb went to business at the customary hour, but returned early in the afternoon to attend some public meeting in Westminster, connected with politics. Influential people—Conservatives: who were called Tories then—had for some time past been soliciting him to go into Parliament; he had not quite made up his mind yet whether he would, or not.

He and his wife dined alone. Lord and Lady Kingdon, with whom they were intimate, were to have dined with them; but only a few minutes before the time of sitting down, a note came to say they had received

ill news of one of their children, who was at
school at Twickenham, and had to hasten
thither. Adela was tryingly cross and contrary at table: she had not wished to be
alone with her husband, lest he should have
found out what she had done, and begin upon
it. So, after the first few minutes, the meal
proceeded nearly in silence. She did not
fear the explosion quite as much as she did
at first: each hour as it went on smoothly,
helped to make her uneasiness less.

But she was not to escape long. Just as
the servants were quitting the room, leaving
the wine on the table, one of them came back.
again.

"Mr. Howard has called, sir. He says
he would not disturb you at this hour, but he
must see you on a matter of pressing business."

"Pressing business!" echoed Mr. Grubb.
"Show Mr. Howard in. A chair, Richard,
and glasses."

The stiff and stern old man entered, bowing
to Lady Adela. His iron-grey hair looked
greyer than usual, and his black coat rusty.

Rusty coats are worn by more than one millionaire.

"Why, Howard, this is quite an event for you! Why did you not come in time for dinner? Sit down. Anything new? Anything happened?"

"Why, yes," replied Mr. Howard, who was a slow-speaking man, giving one the idea that the bump of caution must be large on his head. "Thank you, port."

"What is it?" inquired the senior partner.

"I will enter upon the matter presently," replied James Howard, deliberately sipping his wine. By which answer Mr. Grubb of course understood that he would only speak when they were alone:

Lady Adela swallowed her strawberries and left her seat so quickly that Mr. Grubb could hardly get to the door in time to open it, and she went up to the drawing-room. She felt sure, as sure as though she could read his very thoughts, that "that horrid Howard" had come about the cheque. She did not care so much that her husband should find it out; he might do his best and his worst, and the worst from him she did not dread greatly; but that that old ogre should know it, perhaps take steps—oh, that was quite another thing. *Could* he take steps ?—would the law justify it ? Adela did not know; but she began to give the reins to her imagination, and cowered in terror.

As she thus sat, her ears painfully alive to every sound, a cab rattled into the square, and stopped at the door. It brought Charles Cleveland. Charley had just come up from Netherleigh; the train was late, and he was in a desperate hurry to get into his dress-clothes, to attend a " spread "—it was what Charley called it—given by his brother. Adela ran out, and arrested him as he was making for his room, three stairs at a time.

" Charley, I want to speak to you—just for a moment. What mortal haste you are in ! "

To be invited thus into the drawing-room by her, to meet her again after this temporary absence, was to him as light breaking in upon darkness. " Oh Charles," she added, giving him both her hands, in the moment's agitation, "surely some good fairy sent you! I am in distress."

"Can I soothe it?" he asked, wondering at her emotion, and retaining her hands in his. "Can I do anything for you?"

"I am in sore need of a friend—to—to shelter me," she continued. "Great, desperate need!"

"Can I be that friend? Suffer me if you can. *Suffer* me to be, Lady Adela. Dear! dear! what can have happened?"

"But it may bring danger upon you, difficulty, even disgrace. I believe I ought not to ask it of you."

"Danger and difficulty would be welcome, borne for you," returned Charley in his loyalty. "Believe that, Lady Adela."

He could not imagine what was amiss, and he caught somewhat of her agitation. That she was in real trouble, nay, in terror, was all too plain. For a moment the thought occurred—was Mr. Grubb angry with her on his account? Oh, what a privilege it appeared to him, foolish but honest-hearted fellow, to be asked to shield her!

"I will trust you," she cried, her emotion increasing. "That cheque—but oh, Charles, do not you think ill of me! It was done in a moment of irritation."

"Say on, dear Lady Adela."

"That cheque—he did not give it me. I had asked for money, and he refused. I wanted it badly; and I was angry with him: *so I drew out the cheque.*"

Charley felt all at sea, not comprehending in the least. She saw it: and was forced to go on with her painful explanation. The colour was coming and going in her cheek; now white as a lily, now rose-red.

"That cheque you cashed for me on Saturday morning, Charley. Mr. Grubb did not draw it. Mr. Howard's name was signed as well as his; and—and he is with my husband in the dining-room, and I am frightened to death."

There was a momentary pause. Charley understood now, and saw all the *difficulty* of the matter, as she had lightly called it. But his honest love for her was working strongly in his heart, and he formed a hasty, chivalrous resolve to shield her if he could. Had she not appealed to him?

"I want you not to say that it was from me you had the cheque, Charley."

"I never will say it. Rely upon me."

"They cannot *do* anything to me, I suppose; or to anyone else," she went on. "It is the exposure that would drive me wild. I could not bear that even that old Howard should know it was I. Oh, Charles, what can be done?"

"Be at ease, Lady Adela. You shall never repent your confidence. Not a breath of suspicion shall come near you. I will shield you; I am proud to do it; shield you, if need be, with my life. You little know how valueless that life would be without your society, dear Lady Adela."

"Now Charles, hold your tongue. You must not take to say such things to me. They are not right—and are all nonsense besides. What would Mr. Grubb think?"

"Forgive me," murmured Charley, all repentance. "I did not mean to say aught that was disloyal to him or you, Lady Adela:

I could not be capable of it, now, or ever. And I will keep my word—to shield you · through this trouble. I repeat it. I swear it."

He wrung her hand in token of good faith, and escaped to prepare for his engagement. She sat down, somewhat reassured, but not at all easy in her conscience. The world just now seemed rather hard to the Lady Adela.

CHAPTER VII.

GIVEN INTO CUSTODY.

THEY sat at the well-spread dessert-table in Grosvenor Square, those two gentlemen, the sole partners of almost the wealthiest house in London; keen, honourable, first-rate men of business, yet presenting somewhat of a contrast in themselves. He at the table's head, Francis Grubb, was fine and stately, wearing in his countenance, in its expression of form and feature, the impress of true nobility—nature's nobility, not that of the peerage—and young yet. James Howard, who might be called the chief partner, so far as work and constant, regular attendance in the City went, though he did not receive anything like an equal share of the profits, was an elderly man, high-shouldered, his face hard and stern, his hair iron grey, and his black coat rusty. Mr. Howard had walked up

from his house in Russell Square this evening
to confer with his chief upon some matter of
business. It a little surprised Mr. Grubb:
for, with them, business discussions were
always confined to their legitimate province—
the City.

The Lady Adela, Mr. Grubb's rebellious
but very charming wife, quitted the room
speedily, leaving them to the discussion that
Mr. Howard had intimated he wished for.
But Mr. Howard did not show himself in any
haste to enter upon it. He sat on, surveying
abstractedly the glittering table before him,
with its rich cut glass, its silver, its china,
and its sweet flowers, talking—abstractedly
also—of the passing topics of the day, more
particularly of a political meeting which had
taken place that afternoon. Mr. Grubb was
a Conservative; he a Liberal; or, as it was
more often styled in those days, Tory and
Whig.

"What news is it that you have brought
me, Howard?" began Mr. Grubb at last,
breaking a pause of silence.

"Aye—my news," returned Mr. Howard,

as though recalled to the thought. "Did you draw a cheque on Saturday morning, before leaving home, in favour of self, and get it cashed at Glyn's?"

Mr. Grubb threw his thoughts back on Saturday morning. The reminiscence was unpleasant. The scene which had taken place with his wife was painful to him, disgraceful to her. He had drawn no cheque.

"No," he answered, thinking a vast deal more of that scene than of Mr. Howard's question.

"A cheque for five hundred pounds, in favour of self?" continued Mr. Howard, slowly sipping his port wine.

"I don't draw at Glyn's in favour of self. You know that, Howard, as well as I do." Messrs. Glyn and Co. were the bankers of the firm; Coutts and Co. the private bankers of Mr. Grubb.

"Just so. Therefore, upon the fact coming to our notice this afternoon that such a cheque had been drawn and paid, I stepped over to Glyn's and made inquiries."

"How did it come to your notice?"

" This way. John Strasfield had all the cheques, drawn last week, sent to him for the usual purpose of verification—he has his own ways of doing his business, you know. In looking over them he was rather struck with this cheque, because it was drawn to self. Self, too ; not selves. After regarding it for a minute or two, another thought struck him —that the signature was not quite like yours. So he brought the cheque to me. I don't think you signed it."

Mr. Grubb rose and closed the door, which he had left ajar after opening it for Lady Adela, the evening being very warm. John Strasfield was their confidential cashier in Leadenhall Street.

" If it is your signature, your hand must have been nervous when you wrote it," continued Mr. Howard, " rendering the letters less decided than usual."

That Mr. Grubb had been nervous on Saturday morning he was quite conscious of ; though not, he believed, to the extent of making his hand unsteady. But he had not drawn any cheque.

" It was drawn in favour of self, you say. Was it signed with my private signature, Francis C. C. Grubb ? "

" No ; with the firm's signature, Grubb and Howard. Glyn's people suspected nothing wrong, and cashed it."

" Who presented the cheque ? "

" Charles Cleveland. And he received the money."

" Charles Cleveland ! " repeated Mr. Grubb in surprise, his whole attention fully aroused now. " There is some mystery about this."

" So it seemed to me," answered the elder man. " Cleveland stayed out of town to-day—by your leave I think you said."

" Yes, he asked me on Saturday to let him have to-day ; he was going down to Netherleigh : his elder brother, Captain Cleveland, meant to run down there to say good-bye. Charles will be back to-night, I suppose. But—I don't understand about this cheque."

" I'm sure I don't," said Mr. Howard. " Except that Charles Cleveland got it cashed."

" Where did Charles Cleveland procure the

cheque?" asked Mr. Grubb, his head all in a puzzle. "Who drew the cheque? Where's the money? Howard, there must be some mistake in your information."

"It was Saturday morning that you left the cheque-book at home, and sent Cleveland for it, if you remember," said Mr. Howard, quietly.

"Ah, to be sure it was; I do remember. A long while he was gone."

"You asked him what made him so long. I chanced to be in your room at the moment: and he said he had been doing a little errand for himself. Well, during that period of his absence, that is, somewhere between ten and half-past eleven, the cheque was presented by him at Glyn's, and cashed. What does it all say?" concluded Mr. Howard.

Francis Grubb looked a little bewildered. No clear idea upon the point was suggesting itself to his mind.

"I thought young Cleveland was given to improvident habits," resumed Mr. Howard, "but I never suspected he was one to help himself to money in this way; to——"

"He *cannot* have done it," interrupted Mr. Grubb, earnestly decisive. "It is quite impossible. Charles Cleveland is foolish and silly enough, just as boys will be, for he is no better than a boy; but he is honest and honourable."

"Are you aware that he spends a great deal of money?"

"I think he does. I said so to him last week. It was that pouring wet day, Wednesday, I think, and I told him he might go down to Leadenhall Street with me in the carriage if he liked. I took the opportunity of speaking to him about his expenditure, telling him it was a great deal easier to get into debt than to get out of it."

"Which he had found out for himself, I expect," grumbled Mr. Howard. "How did he receive it?"

"As ingenuously as you could wish. Blushed like a school-girl. He confessed that he had been spending too much money lately, and laid it chiefly to the score of his brother's being in London. Captain Cleveland's comrades are rather an expensive set;

the allowance that he gets from his uncle is good ; and Charles has been led into expense through mixing with them. The very moment his brother left, he said, he should draw in and spend next to nothing.''

Mr. Howard smiled grimly. ''One evening, strolling out after my dinner, I chanced to meet the young gentleman, came full upon him as he was turning out of a florist's, a big bouquet of white flowers in his hand. 'You must have given a guinea for that, young sir,' I said to him, and he did not deny it; just leaped into a cab and was off. I don't suppose those flowers were presented to Captain Cleveland or to any of his comrades.''

Mr. Grubb knitted his brow. He had not the slightest doubt they were intended for his wife. What a silly fellow that Charley was !

'' He may get into debt; I feel sure he is in debt ; but he would not commit forgery—or help himself to money that was not his. I tell you, Howard, the thing is impossible.''

'' He presented the cheque and received the money,'' dryly remarked Mr. Howard. ''What has he done with it ? ''

"But no one, not even a madman, would go to work in this barefaced way," contended his more generous-minded partner, "conscious that it must bring immediate detection and punishment down upon his head."

"Detection, yes; punishment does not necessarily follow. That, he may be already safe from."

"How do you mean?"

"Suppose you inquire what clothes he took with him," suggested Mr. Howard. "My impression is that he's off. Gone. The Netherleigh tale may have been only a blind."

Mr. Grubb rose and rang the bell, staggered nearly out of his senses; and, until it was answered, not another word was spoken. Each gentleman was busy with his own thoughts.

"Richard," began the master to his servant, "when Mr. Charles Cleveland left for the country yesterday morning, did he take much luggage with him?"

"Don't think he took any, sir; unless it was his small portmanteau."

"Did you happen to hear him say whether he intended to make a long stay?"

"I did not hear him say anything, sir: he went out early, to catch the first train. But Mr. Cleveland is back."

"Back!" echoed Mr. Howard, surprised into the interference.

"Yes, sir, just now, and went out again as soon as he had dressed. He is gone to dine at the Army and Navy."

"Then no elucidation can now take place until morning," observed Mr. Grubb, as the servant withdrew. "When he has gone out lately on these dining bouts he does not get home till late, sometimes not at all. But rely upon it, Howard, this matter will be cleared up satisfactorily, so far as he is concerned. Though what the mystery attending the cheque can be, I am not able to imagine."

"I'm sure I am not, looking at it from your point of view," returned the elder man. "See here: you come down to Leadenhall Street on Saturday morning, and find you have left the cheque-book of the firm at home here. You send Charles Cleveland for it, telling him to take a cab and to make haste. After being away three or four times as long as he need be, he comes back with the cheque-book, having found it, he says, where you had told him it probably would be found—in the room where you breakfasted. He does not account for his delay, except by the excuse that he was doing an errand for himself, and begs pardon for it. Well and good. To-day we find that a cheque has been abstracted from that same cheque-book, filled in for five hundred pounds, and was cashed by Cleveland himself, all during this same interval on Saturday morning when he declines to account for his time. What do you make of it?"

Put thus plainly before him, Mr. Grubb did not know what to make of it, and his faith in Charles Cleveland began to waver. The most prejudiced mind cannot altogether fight against palpable facts. Mr. Howard opened his pocket-book, took the cheque in question from it, and laid it, open, before his senior partner.

"This is not Cleveland's writing," remarked Mr. Grubb.

"Of course not. It is an imitation of yours. That is, not his ordinary handwriting.

He has done it pretty cleverly. Glyns were deceived. Not but that I consider Glyns' clerk was incautious not to see the difference between ' self' and ' selves.' He says he did not notice the word at all : but he ought to have noticed it."

" It is a singular affair altogether," observed Mr. Grubb, in a musing tone. " To begin with, my bringing home the cheque-book at all was singular. You were not in the City on Friday, you know, Howard, and ——"

" I couldn't come when I was ill," grunted out Mr. Howard.

" My dear, good old friend, do you suppose I thought you could ?" answered Mr. Grubb, checking a laugh. " I was going to say that, as you were absent, I signed the cheques on Friday, and the book lay on my desk. It happened that my private cheque-book also lay there. When I left, I put the firm's cheque-book in my pocket by mistake, and locked up the other ; meaning, of course, to do just the contrary. But for this carelessness on my part, Charles Cleveland would not have had the opportunity of —— Good heavens! what a blow this will be for his father! We must hush it up!"

"Hush it up!" cried out the other and sterner man of business. "Not if I know it. That's just like you, Francis Grubb! Your Uncle Francis, my many years' friend, used to accuse you, you know, of having a soft place in your heart."

"I am thinking of that good man, with his many cares, the Rector of Netherleigh."

"And I am thinking of his son's bold, bare-faced iniquity. Be you very sure of one thing, sir — Glyns won't hush it up; they are the wrong people to do it. Neither must you. A pretty example it would be! No, thank you, no more wine; I have had my quantity."

"Well, well, we shall see, Howard. I cannot understand it yet."

When Mr. Grubb got upstairs that night, he found his wife gone out, leaving no message for him. She never did leave any. Davvy thought her lady had gone to the opera. Mr. Grubb followed, and found her there. The box was full, and there was little room for him. He said nothing to her of what had occurred : he meant to keep it from her if he could, to save her pain ; and from all others, for the Honourable and Reverend Mr. Cleveland's sake.

Mr. Grubb sat down to breakfast the next morning alone. Lady Adela had not risen ; Charles Cleveland did not make his appearance.

" Does Mr. Charles Cleveland know I am at breakfast, Hilson ? " he inquired of the butler, who was in attendance.

" Mr. Charles Cleveland left word—I beg your pardon, sir, I forgot to mention it—that he has gone out to breakfast with his brother, Captain Cleveland, who sails to-day for India. He went out between six and seven."

" He came home last night, then ? "

" Yes, sir ; about one o'clock."

Mr. Grubb glanced over the letters waiting in a stack by his plate, some for himself, some for Lady Adela. Amidst the former was one from his sister, written on Saturday. Her mother (who had been seriously ill for some time) was much worse, she said, and she begged her brother to come down, if possible, on Monday morning.

It chanced that Mr. Grubb had made one or two appointments for people to see him that morning at his house; so that it was eleven o'clock when he reached Leadenhall Street.

"Well, where is he?" began Mr. Howard, without ceremony of greeting.

"Where's who?" asked Mr. Grubb.

"Charles Cleveland."

"What—is he not come yet?" returned Mr. Grubb, whose thoughts had been elsewhere.

"Not yet. I don't think he means to."

To be late, or in any other way inattentive to his duties, had not been one of Charley's sins. Therefore his absence was the more remarkable. Mr. Grubb started for Blackheath, almost endorsing Mr. Howard's opinion that the delinquent had embarked with his brother for India, or some other place not speedily accessible to officers of justice.

Twelve o'clock was striking by St. Paul's when Charley bustled in, hot, and out of

breath.   He was told that Mr. Howard
wanted him.

"I beg your pardon, sir, for being so
late," he panted, addressing himself to that
gentleman, when he reached his private room,
"especially after my holiday of yesterday.
I went early this morning to Woolwich, and
on board ship with my brother, intending to
be back by business hours ; but, what with
one delay and another, I was unable to get
up till now."

"It is not business-like at all, sir," growled
the old merchant.   "But—stay a bit, Mr.
Cleveland ; we have a few questions to put to
you."

Charles glanced round.   In his hurry he
had seen no one but Mr. Howard.   His eye
now fell on a little man, who sat in a corner.
Charley knew him to be connected with
Glyn's house ; and he knew that the time
was at hand when he would have need of all
his presence of mind and his energies.   It
chanced that this gentleman had just called
to enquire if anything had come to light about
the mysterious cheque.

"You presented a cheque for five hundred pounds at Glyn's on Saturday morning, and received the amount in notes," began Mr. Howard, to Charles. "From whom did you get that cheque?"

No reply.

"Purporting to be drawn and signed by Mr. Grubb. I ask from whom you received it?"

"I decline to answer," Charles said at length, speaking with hesitation, in spite of his preparation for firmness.

"Do you deny having presented the cheque?"

"No. I do not deny that."

"Do you deny having received the money for it?" interposed the gentleman from the bank.

"Nor that, either. I acknowledge to have received five hundred pounds. It would be a waste of folly to deny it," continued Charles to him, in a sort of calm desperation, "since your clerk could prove the contrary."

"But did you know what you were laying yourself open to?" cried Mr. Howard, evidently in a marvel of astonishment, for he

took these admissions of Charles's to be tanta-
mount to an absolute acknowledgment of his
guilt.

" I know now, sir."

" Will you refund the money ? " asked Mr.
Howard, dropping his voice ; for that stern
man of business had been going over the
affair half the night as he lay in bed, and
concluded to give the reckless young fellow a
chance. Truth to say, Mr. Howard's bark
was always worse than his bite. "Out of
consideration for your family, connected, as
it is, with that of the head of our firm, we
are willing to be lenient ; and if you will
confess, and refund —— "

" I cannot refund, and I must decline to
answer any more questions," interrupted
Charles, fast relapsing into agitation.

Mr. Howard stared at him. " Do you
understand, young man, what it is that you
would bring upon your head ? In point of
fact we are laying ourselves open to, I hardly
know what penalty of law, in making you
this offer ; but Mr. Grubb is anxious it
should be hushed up for your father's sake —

whom everybody respects. If you decline it; if you set me at defiance, as it seems to me you wish to do; I shall have no resource but to give you into custody."

"I beg to state that the matter is not in our hands yet," spoke up the banker to Charles. "If it were, we could not make you any such offer. Though of course we can fully understand and appreciate the motives that actuate your principals, with whom the affair at present wholly rests. It would be a terrible blow to fall on the Cleveland family; and everyone must wish to save them from it."

"I—I am very sorry," gasped Charles, feeling all this to his heart's core. " Unfortunately ——— "

"The matter is not known beyond ourselves," interposed Mr. Howard again, indicating himself and the banker; " and it need not be. But it is solely out of consideration for your family, you understand, that we offer to hush it up. Will you explain? "

" I cannot. Unfortunately, I cannot, sir. It is not in my power."

"Then I give you in charge at once."

"I can't help it," said poor Charles, passing his hand over his hot brow.

Mr. Howard, very hard, very uncompromising when deliberately provoked, was as good as his word. And Charles Cleveland was given into custody for forgery.

CHAPTER VIII.

"THAT IT MAY BE WELL WITH US IN AFTER LIFE."

IT was all over and done with long before Mr. Grubb got up from Blackheath in the afternoon. He felt terribly vexed. Vexed for Charles himself, terribly vexed for Charles's family, vexed on his own score. To his refined and sensitive mind, it almost seemed that he had violated the sacred laws of hospitality, for Charles had been staying, as a guest, in his house.

The first thing he did was to hasten to the prison to which Charles had been conveyed, preparatory to his examination on the morrow. The young man was in his cell, sitting on the edge of his narrow bed, and looking very downhearted. The entrance of Mr. Grubb seemed to bring to him a sudden flash of hope. He started up.

"Oh, sir," he exclaimed, in high excitement, "will you not look over this one error? My father will replace the money—I am sure he will, rather than suffer this public disgrace to fall upon the family. Do not force the shame upon him. And—and there's my brother—just embarked—what will he do? Oh, Mr. Grubb, if you will but have mercy!"

"Charles—don't excite yourself like this—I am come here to offer you the mercy," spoke Mr. Grubb; and his considerate manner, his voice of music, were just like a healing balm. "I am come straight from Mr. Howard to renew the offer he made you. It is not yet too late: we will make things right to-morrow: there will be no prosecutor, you understand. Will you give me, myself only, the particulars you denied to Mr. Howard?"

Just for one eager moment the wish flashed across Charles's mind that he might tell the truth to this good man. Was he not Adela's husband, and would he not excuse her in his love? The next, he saw how futile was the wish. Could *he* be the one to betray her?— and to her husband? Shame upon him for the thought! He had vowed to her to hold her harmless, and he would do so for her sake.

" To me it appears that there's a mystery in the affair which I cannot fathom," continued Mr. Grubb. " Your conduct in it is perfectly incomprehensible. It may be better for you to confide in me, Charles."

" I cannot, sir. I wish I could."

" What if I tell you that, in spite of appearances, I do not myself believe you guilty ? "

A bright, eager flush, a glance as of mutual *understanding* illumined for a moment Charley's face. It seemed to say that just, honourable natures know and trust in each other's innocence, no matter what may be the surrounding signs of guilt. But the transient expression faded away to sadness, and Mr. Grubb was in doubt whether it had really been there.

" I can explain nothing," said the prisoner. " I can only thank you, sir, for this proof of confidence, and implore your clemency on the ground of compassion alone."

" Charles Cleveland, this won't do. You are either guilty or innocent. Which is it ? "

"Guilty, of course," said Charley in his desperation. For if he said "innocent," the next rejoinder would be "Then who is guilty?" And he could not answer that, or any other close question.

"Did you do this vile thing of your own accord; or were you induced to do it by another?" pursued Mr. Grubb, his head running upon Charley's debts and Charley's fast companions.

"I—I—pray do not ask me more, sir! It is a wretched business, and I must suffer for it."

"Am I to understand that you wholly refuse to confide in me?—refuse to be helped? I would be your true friend."

"I must refuse," gasped poor Charley. "I have nothing to tell. I did present the cheque at Glyn's, and I drew the money. And—and I hope you will forgive me, sir, for I am very miserable."

"Is all the money spent?"

"I—I have not got as much as a shilling of it. If I had, I'd give it back. It's too late."

Nothing better than this could Mr. Grubb

wring from the unfortunate prisoner. And he left him *believing he was guilty.* He left in rather an angry mood, too, for he thought Charles was bearing out Mr. Howard's report and showing himself defiantly, ungratefully obstinate. That he had been in some most pressing and perhaps dangerous difficulty on the Saturday morning, and had used these desperate means to extricate himself, must be, he concluded, the fact. A great deal of his compassion for Charles melted away; the young man seemed hardened.

On the following morning the case was taken before the magistrates. It was heard in private. The influential house, Grubb and Howard, could have commanded a greater concession than that. One magistrate only sat, a very pliable one, Sir Turtle Kite. The case was but slightly gone into, the prosecutors asking for a week's remand : they wished to trace out more particulars, also wished to trace the notes. At the end of that time the prisoner would be brought up again; and meanwhile he was consigned to that awful place, Newgate.

In spite of all efforts to keep it secret, the affair partially got wind. Not, however, in its true details. All kinds of exaggerated rumours and surmises ran the rounds of the clubs. But for the recent sojourn of Captain Cleveland in London, Charley might have remained quite an obscure individual, as regarded the fashionable world. But he had been a great deal with his brother, and was known and liked everywhere.

What a commotion arose! Charles Cleveland in Newgate on a charge of robbery, or forgery, or what not! Charley Cleveland the popular,—Charley Cleveland, the grandson of an earl gathered to his fathers, and nephew of one who stood in his shoes,— Charley Cleveland, the out-and-out good fellow, who was wont to scare the blue devils away from everybody,—Charley Cleveland, who, in defiance of his improvidence and his shallow pocket, was known to be of the nicest honour amongst the honourable!

"The thing's preposterous altogether," stuttered John Cust, who had a natural stammer. "If Charley had drawn the money he

would have had the money, and I know that
on Saturday afternoon he had not a rap, for he
borrowed three sovs. of me to take him down
to Brighton ———"

"Netherleigh, Cust."

"Netherleigh, then. What put Brighton in
my head, I wonder? Fancy he went to try
to get some money out of his governor."

"Which he did," added Lord Deerhum.
" A five-pound note."

"And paid me back the three sovs. on
the Monday night, when he came to his
brother's spread at the Rag and Famish,"
continued John Cust. "Gammon! Charley
has not been making free with anybody's
name."

"But he acknowledges to having drawn
the money," squeaked Booby Charteries. "A
thousand pounds, they say,"

"You may take that in yourself, Booby.
We don't."

"But the Lord Mayor ———"

"Lord Mayor be hanged! If he swears
till he's black in the face that Charley did it,
I know he didn't. There."

" 'Twasn't the Lord Mayor. Some other one of those City big-wigs."

" Anyway, he is in Newgate. It's said, too, that it is Grubb and Howard who have sent him there."

" Did he rob their cash-box ? "

" Do they accuse him of it, you mean, Booby: As if Charley would do such a thing ! "

" Let us go down to Newgate, and have a smoke with him," cried Charteries, who had so small a share of brains and so very small a voice as to have acquired the nickname Booby: " It may cheer the young fellow up, under the present alarming state of things."

" As if they'd admit us inside Newgate, or a smoke either ! " retorted John Cust. " There's only one thing more difficult than getting into Newgate, and that is, if you are in, getting out again. Don't forget that, Booby."

" Couldn't some of us go and punch a few heads down there, beginning with old Howard's," again proposed Booby. " I don't say Grubb's."

"Grubb has had nothing to do with bringing the charge; you may rely upon that," said Lord Deerhum. "Grubb's a gentleman. You shut up, Booby."

Ah! it was all very well for these idle, foolish young men to express their sympathy with the prisoner in their idle, foolish way: but, what of the distress of those connected with him?

Thomas Cleveland, Honourable and Reverend, heard from his wife, who was still staying at her mother's, that something was amiss, and came up from Netherleigh to find his son incarcerated in Newgate and accused of forgery. Down he went to the prison at once, and got admission. Charley looked, in that short period, greatly changed. His dress was neglected, his hair unkempt, and his face haggard. Charley, the fastidious!

Mr. Cleveland was overcome beyond control, and sobbed aloud. He was a venerable-looking man of nearly sixty years now, and had always been a fond father. Charley was little less affected.

"Why did you not kill me when you last

came down, Charles?" he moaned out in his perplexity and anguish. "Better have put me out of this world of pain than bring this misery upon me. Oh, my boy! my boy! you were your mother's favourite: how can you so have disgraced her memory?"

"I would I had been put out of the world, rather than be the curse to you I have proved," writhed Charley, wishing Newgate would yawn asunder and engulph him. "Oh, don't —father, don't!" he implored, as Mr. Cleveland's sobs echoed through the cell. "If it will be any consolation to you to know it, I will avow to you that I am not guilty," he added, the sight of his father's affliction momentarily outweighing his precaution. "By all your care of me, by your present grief, by the memory of my dead mother, I swear to you that I am not guilty."

Mr. Cleveland looked up, and his heart leaped within him. He knew Charles was speaking truth. It was impossible to mistake that earnest tone.

"Thank God!" he murmured. "But what, then, is this I hear, about your declining to make a defence ? " he presently asked. " I am told you have as good as acknowledged your guilt." Charles hung his head, and relapsed into prudence again.

" My boy, answer me. How came you to accept—as it were—the charge, if you are innocent ? "

" For your private comfort I have said this, dear father, but it must remain between us as if it had not been spoken. The world must still, and always, believe me guilty."

" But why ?—why ? What mystery is this ? "

" Do not ask me, sir. Believe that you have not a son more free from the guilt of this crime than I am. Nevertheless, I must pay the penalty, for I cannot defend myself."

Mr. Cleveland thought this about the most extraordinary thing he had ever met with. Nothing more could he get out of Charles ; nevertheless, he did believe in his innocence. From Newgate he went on to Leadenhall Street, to see the gentlemen who had brought this charge, and found only one of them in : Mr. Grubb.

"You are not more pained at the affair than I am," said the latter, closing the door of his private room, " and certainly not more astonished."

"Oh, Mr. Grubb," cried the clergyman, "could you not have hushed this wretched disgrace up, for all our sakes? ——or at least made more inquiries before taking these extreme steps? You who have shown so much true friendship for me!"

"I would have hushed it up. I wished to hush it up altogether. I would have paid the money over and over again out of my own pocket, rather than it should have become known, even to Mr. Howard. It was he, however, who brought the tidings of it to me."

"And Mr. Howard would not?"

"Mr. Howard would. At first he seemed inclined to be hard. Thorough business men look upon these things with a stern eye. However, he knew my wishes, and came to. He was the first to speak to Charles. He asked him to acknowledge the truth to him, and he would forgive it. Charles refused; set him, so to say, at defiance; told him, I

believe, to do his best and his worst ; and Mr.
Howard gave him into custody."

" It is very strange."

" When I found what had happened—I
had been out of town that day—I went at
once to Charles. I told him that I could
not believe him guilty, and I entreated him to
tell me the circumstances of the case, which
looked to me then, and looks still, unaccount-
ably mysterious ———"

" And he would not ? " interrupted Mr.
Cleveland, recalling how Charles had just met
a similar request from himself.

" He would not tell me a word : told me
he would not. I said I could even then set
matters straight, and would get his release on
the morrow, and nothing about it should ever
transpire. He thanked me, but said he had
nothing to tell ; was, in fact, guilty. I could
only think he must be guilty, and left him
with that impression on my mind."

" It is altogether very strange," repeated
Mr. Cleveland in a musing tone, as he sat
stroking his face and thinking. " Will you
state the particulars to me, as far as you are

cognisant of them. I asked Charles to do so, but he would not."

"It occurred on Saturday morning," began Mr. Grubb. "When I reached the City here, I found I had not got with me the cheque-book of the firm, which I had taken away by mistake the previous evening; and I sent Charles home to look for it. He was a long while gone, but brought it when he came. During the period of his absence one of the cheques was abstracted, filled up for five hundred pounds, and ——"

"Filled up by whom?"

"The writing was an imitation of mine. Charles presented it at Glyns', and got it cashed. All this he acknowledges to; but he refuses to say what he did with the money."

"Mr. Grubb," cried the agitated father, "appearances are against him—were never, I perceive, more strongly against anyone; but, before heaven I believe him to be innocent."

Mr. Grubb made no reply.

"He has assured me of his innocence by the memory of his dead mother; and innocent I am sure he must be. He stated in the same breath that he should avow it to no one else, but submit to the penalty of the crime just as though he had committed it. As to what he did with the money—he could not have used it for himself. On that very Saturday afternoon he had to borrow money to bring him down to Netherleigh the next morning. John Cust lent it him."

"It is very singular," acknowledged Mr. Grubb.

"Charles confessed as much to me at Netherleigh—that he had borrowed the money from Cust to get down with; three pounds, I think it was. I gave him a five-pound note, and a lecture with it. He promised to be more cautious for the future, and said that after Harry left he should not have occasion to spend much—which is true. But now, what I would like to know is this—if he drew that five hundred pounds, where is it? How came it that the next hour, so to say, he had none in his pocket?"

Mr. Grubb certainly could not answer, and remained silent.

"Has he been made the instrument of

another?" returned Mr. Cleveland. "Was he imposed upon by anyone ?—sent to cash a cheque that he himself thought was a genuine and proper cheque?"

"That is scarcely likely. Were it the case, what objection could he have to declare it? My opinion is—I am sorry to have to give it—that Charles had got into some desperate money trouble, and used desperate remedies to extricate himself."

"What more desperate trouble could he be in than this?"

"True. But he may have hoped we should be lenient. Even now," added Mr. Grubb, his voice trembling with the concern he felt, "we might be able to save him if he would but disclose the truth. Mr. Howard absolutely refuses to quash the matter unless he does: and I think he is right."

"But Charles won't disclose it; he won't," bewailed the clergyman, taking the other's hand in token of his gratitude. "Look here, my dear friend," he added, after a pause of thought, "can Charles be holding his tongue to screen somebody?"

" To screen somebody ?   How ? "

" That he did this thing willingly, with his eyes open, I never will believe.   It is not in a Cleveland's nature to commit a crime.   Moreover, I repeat to you that he has just assured me of his innocence by the memory of his dead mother.   No, no ; whatever may be the facts, Charles was not wilfully guilty.   I could stake my life upon it.   In cashing that cheque he must have been made the innocent tool of another, whom he won't betray out of some chivalrous feeling of honour."

" But no one had possession of the cheque-book but Charles," reasoned Mr. Grubb. " He found it in the breakfast-room where I had left it.   My servants are honest ; they would not touch it.   Moreover, it was Charles, himself, who presented the cheque for payment, and got the money."

Mr. Cleveland rubbed his grey hair back with a look of perplexity ; hair that was getting scanty now.   Look at the case in what way he would, it presented contradictions and difficulties that seemed to be insuperable.

" You are staying at Lord Acorn's, I sup-

pose," remarked Mr. Grubb, when the clergyman rose to leave.

"Until Saturday. I can't run away from
London and leave my boy in Newgate.
Heaven be with you! I know you'll do for
him what you can."

The whole of the after-part of this day
certain words spoken by the unhappy father
haunted Francis Grubb. *In cashing that
cheque he must have been made the innocent tool
of another, whom he won't betray, out of some
chivalrous feeling of honour.* An idea had been
presented to him which he might never have
taken up of himself; a painful idea; and, do
what he would, he could not drive it away.
It intruded itself into his business; it followed
him home to dinner; and it worried him
while he ate it. He had not found Lady
Adela at home. She was dining out somewhere. Certainly Mr. Grubb's domestic life
was not a very sociable one. After dinner he
went to his club.

It was eleven o'clock before he got home;
later than he had meant to be, but he did not
expect his wife to be there yet. The butler,

a trustworthy, semi-confidential servant, who had entered the service of the uncle, Francis Grubb, when his present master was a boy, and who had become greatly attached to him, came to the drawing-room to see if anything was wanted.

" Is Lady Adela in ? " asked his master.

" No, sir.　Her ladyship came in not long ago, for a minute or two, and went out again."

"Stay a minute, Hilson," cried Mr. Grubb, as the man was turning away.　" Shut the door.　Carry your memory back to last Saturday.　Did you chance to see Mr. Charles Cleveland come in that morning ? "

"Yes, sir: I was at the front door, talking to one of Lady Acorn's servants, who had brought a parcel for my lady.　Mr. Cleveland jumped out of the cab he was in, and ran past me all in a hurry, saying he had come to look for something the master had left behind him."

" Did he go at once to the room where I breakfasted ? "

" No, sir.　My lady chanced to be descending the stairs at the moment ; Mr. Cleveland went towards her, asking where Mr. Grubb had breakfasted. In a minute or two, it could not have been much more, he came running out again, leaped into the cab, and went away in it at a great rate. That was the first time, sir."

Mr. Grubb lifted his eyes. "The first time! What do you mean?"

"Mr. Charles Cleveland came back again, sir. Not directly; half an hour or three-quarters later it may have been, perhaps more, I had not taken particular note of the time. I was in the hall then, watching John clean the lamp—he has done it slovenly of late. The front door was rung and knocked at as if it was going to be knocked down. I opened it, and Mr. Charles Cleveland rushed past me up to the drawing-room: I never hardly saw anybody in a greater hurry than he seemed to be. He came down again directly, my lady with him, and they went into the break-fast-room. He then ran out to the cab, and drove away at a fiercer rate than before."

"Was it the same cab?"

"Oh, yes, sir. Taking both times together he was not in the house three minutes."

"Not long enough to —— " Mr. Grubb checked himself, and remained silent.

"Not long enough to have drawn a false cheque, sir, when the handwriting has to be studied—as we have been saying below," put in the butler, following too closely his master's thoughts.

Mr. Grubb felt disagreeably startled. "Hilson! what are you saying? *Who* has talked of this below?"

"Only Davvy, sir. She got to know of it this morning, through——well, sir, I believe through a letter that my lady gave her to read."

"But how was that?" questioned Mr. Grubb, in a displeased tone.

"It was through a mistake of my lady's, sir," replied Hilson, dropping his voice. "She had meant to give Davvy a note from Madame Damereau, about the trimming of a dress; instead of that, she gave her one from Lady Grace. Davvy has been uneasy ever since, and she spoke in confidence to me."

"Why uneasy?"

·Well, sir, Davvy thinks it an unpleasant

thing to have happened, especially for us upper servants. The cheque must have been torn out and filled in by somebody."

"Nonsense," interposed Mr. Grubb. "Take care you do not speak of this, Hilson; and caution Davvy."

"No fear of me, sir; you know that. I told Davvy she must have misunderstood Lady Grace's note, and that she must hold her tongue; and I am sure she will. She was very sorry to have read it. She asked my lady's instructions as to the dress, and my lady tossed the note to her, saying she would find them there. Davvy read on to the very end, expecting to come to them. That's how it was, sir."

Mr. Grubb remained on alone, deep in painful thought, his head bent on his hand. His vague suspicions were strengthening— strengthening terribly.

And what of Lady Adela? This could not have been a good time for her—as the children say. Made aware that morning by Grace's letter that Charles was taken into custody, she was seized with terror; and perhaps it was not so much carelessness as utter bewilderment that caused the stupid error of handing the wrong letter to Davvy. Adela saw her father in the course of the day. Too anxious to remain passive, she went out to hear what she could at Lord Acorn's, putting to him a cautious word of inquiry. Lord Acorn made light of the whole business—he did not yet know the particulars. Charley would soon be released, he carelessly said; Grubb would take care of that. As to a little fright, or a short incarceration, it would do Master Charley good—he had been going the pace of late. And this opinion of her father's so completely reassured Lady Adela, that her fears of consequences to Charley subsided; she returned home, took up her visiting, and was her own saucy self again.

She came in early to-night, before twelve o'clock, looking cross. Her husband rose from his chair, and smoothed his troubled face.

" Where have you been, Adela ? "

" To Lady Sanely's : " and the tone of defiance audible in Lady Adela's answer arose from the consciousness that he had forbidden her to go there. The dissatisfied face she brought back with her, and the early hour of her return, seemed to say that she had not met with much pleasure there this evening. Perhaps she had staked, and lost, all the money she had taken; or, perhaps play was not going on that night.

She threw herself into a chair, eating a biscuit she had caught up from a plate on the table, and let her mantle fall from her shoulders. How very pretty she looked! Her dress was white lace, trimmed about with small blush roses; her cheeks wore a lovely flush; a pearl necklace, of priceless value, lay on her fair neck, bracelets to match encircled her slender arms: one of the many magnificent gifts of her fond husband.

"Don't shut the door," cried Adela, tartly, for he had crossed the room to do it. "I'm sure it's hot enough."

"Ah, but I want to say a few words to you," he replied, as he closed it. And the Lady Adela, divining by a subtle instinct which penetrates to us all at odd moments, one cannot tell how or wherefore, that the subject of his "few words" was to be Charley's trouble, and not her transgression as to Lady Sanely's, armed herself for reprisal. Adela never felt sure afterwards that she had not been wicked enough to put up a hasty prayer for aid. Aid to be firm in disguising the truth : aid to blind him as to her share in the past Saturday's exploit, and to strengthen the accusation against Charley. Rising from her seat, she crossed to the nearest window and threw it open, as if needing a breath of the soft midnight air.

"This is a sad business about Charles Cleveland, Adela. I find you know of it."

"Yes," she answered, fanning away a moth that was floating in, attracted by the light. "I hope you are satisfied with your work. You had a paltry spite against him, and you have cast him into Newgate to gratify it."

"Adela, you know better."

"It is enough to ruin his prospects for life. It would ruin some people's—they who are without influential connections. Of course Charley will soon be on his legs again, and laugh at his paltry enemies."

Mr. Grubb put his hand, almost caressingly, on his wife's arm, and caused her to turn her face to him. " Will you tell me what you know of this, my dear ? "

" Tell you what I know of it !—How should I know anything of it ? " she retorted, flirting her costly fan. " Poor Charley may have meant to borrow the money for a day or two—I don't accuse him ; I only say it may have been so—and then to have replaced it : but you and that old kangaroo of a partner of yours have prevented him doing it. To gratify your own revenge you seized upon him before he had time to act, and threw him into that place of crime where men are hung from—Newgate. You did it to bring disgrace upon my family, through my sister Mary."

He did not reply to this : he was accustomed to her unjust accusations.

" Adela," he said, dropping his voice to a whisper, " were you wholly ignorant of this business ? *Who drew the cheque ?* "

She turned round with a start, defiance in her eyes.

" Adela, my wife," he whispered, gently

laying both hands upon her shoulders in his earnestness, " if you had anything to do with this business, if Charles Cleveland was not the guilty party, acknowledge it now. Confide in me for once. I will avert consequences from him and suspicion from you. The secret shall be buried in my breast, and I will never revert to it."

Oh, what possessed her that she did not respond to this loving appeal in time ? Was it pure fright that prevented her ? Shame ? —Shame to have to confess to her guilt ? Any way, she steeled her heart against it. Her lovely features had grown white, and her eyes fell before his. Presently she raised them, flashing with indignation, her tone, her words, as haughty as you please.

" Mr. Grubb, how dare you offer me this insult ? "

" Do not meet me in this way, Adela. I am asking you a solemn question ; remember that there is One above Who will hear and register your answer. Were you the principal in this transaction, and was Cleveland but your agent ? Do not fear to trust me—*your*

husband : you shall have my free forgiveness,
now, beforehand, my shelter, my protection.
Only tell me the truth, as you wish it to be
well with us both in after life."

Again she cowered before his gaze, and
again recovered herself. Could it be that her
better angel was prompting her to the truthful
path ?

" What can possibly have induced you to
put such a question to me ? "

" It is an idea that has forced itself upon
my mind. Without some such explanation
the affair is to me an utter mystery. If
Charles Cleveland ———"

" And don't you think you ought to be
ashamed of yourself ! " she interrupted. " I
rob a bank ! I steal a cheque ! Has it come
to this—that you suspect *me ?* "

" Forgive me, Adela, if I am wrong. Be
it how it may, you should meet me differently.
Oh, my wife, let there be perfect confidence
between us at this moment, on this subject.
Tell me the truth, as before Heaven ! "

" Am I in the habit of telling you untruths ?
I thought the truths I tell you were generally

a little too plain to be pleasant," she added in her bravado. "None but a mean-spirited man could so suspect his wife."

"This is all you have to say to me, Adela —your definite answer?"

"Definite enough," she retorted, with a nervous sob, between a laugh and a cry; for, what with fear and discomfort, she was becoming slightly hysterical.

"I am bound to believe you, Adela," he said, the tears in her eyes disarming his latent doubts. "I do believe you. But ——"

"And now that you have had your say, listen to me," she interrupted, choking down all better feelings and speaking with contemptuous anger. "Never speak on the subject to me again if you would keep up the semblance of peace between us. My spirit is being dangerously aroused against you, Mr. Grubb; not only for this injustice to me, but for your barbarous treatment of poor Charles Cleveland."

Once more, he knew not why or wherefore, something like a doubt returned to Mr. Grubb's mind. He held her before him.

"It has been the truth, Adela?—as I hope, and pray, and trust! I ask it you once again—that it may be well with us in after life."

"Would I trouble myself to tell a falsehood about it to *you?* Do you think I have no feeling—that I should bear such distrust? And if you would recompense me for this mauvais quart d'heure, you will release that poor fellow to-morrow — for his father's sake."

She flung her husband's arm away and quitted the room, leaving him to *his* feelings. Few can imagine them — torn, outraged, thrown back upon his generous heart. But she had certainly managed to dispel his doubts of herself. No guilty woman, as he believed, could have faced it out as she did.

"It must have been Cleveland's own act and deed, and no other person's," he mentally concluded. "What madness could have come over the lad?"

CHAPTER IX.

TRACING THE NOTES.

ONE of the most able counsellors of the day, Mr. Serjeant Mowham, chanced to be intimately acquainted with the Rector of Netherleigh; and the unhappy father despatched him to Newgate, in a friendly, not in a legal capacity, to see what he could do with or for the prisoner.

He could not do much. The old saying, "Tell your whole case to your lawyer and your doctor," is essential advice, but Charles Cleveland would tell nothing, neither truth nor falsehood. In vain Serjeant Mowham protested, with tears in his eyes (a stock of which, so the Bar affirmed, he kept in readiness), that he was working in the dark, working for pure friendship's sake, and that without some clue or hint to go upon, no defence that had a chance of success could be made, even though his advocate before the judge told all the *un*truths that ever advocate's tongue gave utterance to. The prisoner was immovable, and Serjeant Mowham in despair.

How matters really would have ended, and whether Mr. Howard would have allowed it to come to trial, cannot be said, had not fortune been kinder to Charles than he was to himself.

One morning, when the days before the prisoner's second examination were growing few, the Earl of Acorn had a slice of luck. He had backed a certain horse at a provincial race meeting, and the horse won. Amongst other moneys that changed hands was a fifty-pound note. An hour after the Earl received it he made his way into his drawing-room in haste, where sat his daughters, Grace, and Mary Cleveland ; the latter with her infant on her lap.

" Mary," cried the Earl, " what were the numbers of the notes paid over to Charles Cleveland at Glyn's ? I partly remember them, but not quite."

" My husband has the numbers," answered

Lady Mary. "But the thing has given me by far too much worry, papa, for me to retain them in my head. I am not sure I ever heard them."

"I have them," interrupted Grace: "I copied them the other day. There was no knowing, I thought, but it might prove useful."

"Quite right, Gracie, girl," said the Earl. "Let's see them. '$\frac{A}{F}$ 3, 0, 2, 5, 5,'" continued Lord Acorn, reading one of the numbers which Lady Grace laid before him. "I thought so. One of these notes has just been paid to me, Mary, by young Waterware."

"Where did he get it?" eagerly inquired Grace.

"I did not ask him. It was only since I left him that I noticed the number. I'll get it out of him by-and-by."

"At once, at once, sir," urged Mary. "Oh, papa, do go to him. I feel *sure* Charles is not guilty."

"No impatience, Mary. Where the deuce am I to pick up Waterware at this time of day. I might as well look for a needle in a bottle of hay. To-night I shall know where to find him."

Chance, however, favoured the Earl. In strolling up St. James's Street, in the afternoon, he met Lord Waterware.

"I say, Waterware," he began, linking his arm in that of the younger peer, "where did you get that fifty-pound note you gave me this morning?"

"Where did I get it? Let's see. Oh, from Nile. He was owing me a hundred, and he paid me yesterday. That fifty, two twenties, and a ten. Why? It's not forged, I suppose," cried the young nobleman, with a yawn.

"Not exactly. Wish I had a handful of them. Good day, I'm going on to Nile's."

Colonel Nile, though addicted to play a little at cards for what he called amusement, and sometimes did it for tolerably high stakes, was a very different man from those other men mentioned in this history — Colonel Haughton and Mr. Piggott, who had led Robert Dalrymple to his ruin. They were professed gamblers, and had disappeared from good society long ago. Colonel Nile was a popular member of it, liked and respected.

Lord Acorn found him at home, walking about in a flowery dressing-gown. He was a middle-aged man and a bachelor, and well off.

"The fifty-pound note I paid over to Waterware," cautiously repeated Colonel Nile, somewhat surprised at the question, and wondering whether random young Waterware had got into any scrape. "Why do you want to know where I got it?"

"Because it is one of the notes that Charley Cleveland is in trouble for; the first of them that has been traced. You must give me the information, Nile, or I shall apply for it publicly."

"Oh, I have no objection in the world," cried the Colonel, determined to afford all that was in his power, and so wash *his* hands of any unpleasantness that might turn up. "I received it at Lady Sanely's loo-table, from —— egad! from your own daughter, Lady Adela."

"From Lady Adela!" echoed the surprised listener.

"From Lady Adela, and nobody else," repeated Colonel Nile, "She paid another fifty to the old Dowager Beck the same evening."

Lord Acorn stared. "But surely they don't play as high as that there!"

"Don't they, though! and higher, too. To tell you the truth, Acorn, it's getting a little too high for prudent people. I, for one, mean to draw in. Old mother Sanely lives but for cards, and she'd stake her head if it were loose. She has the deuce's own luck, though."

With a mental word, sharp and short, given to his daughter Adela for allowing herself to be mixed up in company and amusement such as this, Lord Acorn brought his attention back to the present moment. "Adela gave another fifty-pound note to Lady Beck, you say, the same evening! Do you happen to know its number?"

"Not I," retorted the Colonel, who was not altogether pleased at the questions. "I don't make it my business to pry into notes that do not concern me."

"How long is it ago?"

"I hardly know. Nearly a week, I suppose. It is four or five days since I was first con-

fined to the house with this incipient gout.
I think it was the night before that—Saturday night."

Lord Acorn proceeded straight to Lady
Beck's; and, with much trouble and persuasion, she was induced to exhibit the note
spoken of by Colonel Nile, which was still in
her possession, for, like the Colonel, she had
been ill for some days, so had had no opportunity of playing it away. The old dowager
was verging on her dotage, and could not, at
first, be convinced that the Earl was not going
to take law proceedings against her for win-
ning money of his daughter. He soothed her,
copied the number by stealth, went home, and
compared it with Lady Grace's pocket-book.
It was another of the notes !

" What do you think of it, Grace ?" cried
the Earl, in perplexity. " Can Cleveland
have been owing money to Adela."

"I should imagine not," replied Lady Grace.

" To think she should be such a little fool
as to frequent a place where they play like
that ! "

" But, papa, you knew of it."

" I did not know old Sanely went in for those ruinous stakes. Five pounds, or so, in a night to risk—I thought no worse than that."

Grace understood now. She had deemed her father indifferent. He was then looking at it from one point of view ; she from another.

" It wears a singular appearance," mused the Earl. " To tell you the truth, Grace, I don't like the fact of these notes being traced to Adela. It looks—after the rumour of the absurd flirtation they carried on—almost as if she and Cleveland had gone snacks in the spoil. What now, Gracie ? Are you going to fly ? "

For Lady Grace Chenevix had bounded from her chair in sudden agitation, her arms lifted as if to ward off some dread fear. " Sir ! father ! the thing has become clear to me. That I should not have suspected it before ! ——knowing what I did know."

" Child," he cried, gazing at her in amazement, " what is the matter with you ? "

" Adela did this. I see it all. She drew the cheque. Charles Cleveland was only her instrument ; and, in his infatuated attachment he has taken the guilt on himself, to shield her. Well may he have asserted his innocence to his father! Well may his conduct have appeared to us all so incomprehensible!"

"Why, Grace, you are mad!" gasped the Earl. "Accuse your sister of—of—forgery! Do you reflect on the meaning of your words?"

"Father, do not look so sternly at me. I feel sure I am right. I assure you it is as if scales had fallen from my eyes, for I see it perfectly clear. Adela wanted money for play: she had been drawn in, far deeper than anyone suspected, sir, at Lady Sanely's gaming-table. It was Mr. Grubb's intention to refuse her further funds: no doubt he did refuse them: and ——"

"How do you know it was his intention?"

"Oh, papa, I do know it; never mind how now; I say that Mr. Grubb must have refused her; and she, when this cheque-book fell into her hands ——"

"Don't continue, Grace," sharply interposed Lord Acorn; "you make my blood run cold. You must prove what you assert, or retract it. If—it—is proved"—the Earl drew a long breath—" Cleveland must be extricated. What a thundering fool the fellow must be ? "

" Let me have time to think," said Grace, putting her hand to her head. " Extricated of course he must be, for I know it is true, but —if possible—without exposing Adela."

With the last words, Grace sank back in her chair and burst into a storm of sobs. Lord Acorn was little less moved. They spoke together further, and agreed not to tell Mary Cleveland, in spite of her state of impatience, that Lord Acorn had traced the numbers of the two notes.

Lady Grace decided to confide all to Mr. Grubb. It could not be kept from him long ; and she wanted to bespeak his clemency for Adela. So in the evening she proceeded to his house, tolerably sure that her sister would be out somewhere or other. But she found Mr. Grubb also out : at his club, Hilson thought. Grace dismissed her carriage, went up to the drawing-room, and wrote a word to Mr. Grubb, asking him to come home. The thought crossed her, that perhaps it was not quite the thing to do, but Lady Grace

Chenevix was not the one to stand upon formal ceremony.

He returned at once, full of bustle and looking rather anxious. "Anything the matter, Grace? Anything amiss with Adela? She's not ill?"

"She is at the opera, I fancy; very well, no doubt." And then she sat down and imparted her suspicions — just an allusion to them — that her poor sister was the culprit.

"Grace," he whispered, "I don't mind telling you that the same fear haunted me, and I spoke to her. She indignantly denied it."

"Two of the notes have been traced," murmured Grace.

"Traced!"

"Paid away by Adela, at Lady Sanely's."

There was a dead silence. Lady Grace Chenevix did not raise her eyelids, for she felt keenly the pain of avowal. An ominous shade of despair overspread his face.

"Grace, Grace," he broke forth in anguish, "what is it you are saying?"

"One of them, for fifty pounds, came into

my father's hands to-day, and he has traced it back to Adela," continued Grace, striving to keep down the signs of her pain. "Another of them she paid the same evening to the Dowager Beck. Papa knows of this; he found it out to-day. What inference can we draw but that Adela —— You know what I would say."

"Could she descend to this?" he groaned. "To be a party with Charles Cleveland ——"

"Charles was no party to it," interrupted Grace warmly; "he must have been her instrument, nothing more. Rely upon that. Whatever may be his follies, he is the soul of honour. And it must be from some chivalrous sense of honour, of noblesse oblige, you understand, that he is continuing to shield her now the matter has come out. What is to be done? Charles Cleveland must not be tried as a felon."

"Heaven forbid!—if he be indeed innocent. But, Grace," thoughtfully added Mr. Grubb, "I cannot but think you are mistaken. Were Adela guilty she would have acknowledged it to me, when I assured her in all tenderness that I would forgive, shield, and protect her."

Grace answered by a despairing gesture. "She would not confess to you for very shame, I fear. Dear Mr. Grubb, *what* is to be done? We have to save Adela's good name as well as his. You must see Charles, and get the truth from him."

"I would rather get it from Adela."

"If you can. I doubt it. Having denied it once, she will never confess now."

Lady Grace had reason. Mr. Grubb spoke to his wife the following morning. He said that two of the notes had been traced to her possession; and that, for her own sake, she had better explain, while grace was yet held out to her. But he spoke very coolly, without the smallest sign of endearment or tenderness; nay, there was a suspicion of contempt in his tone, and that put Adela's spirit up.

What answered she? Was she quite blind, quite foolish? She persisted in her denial, called him by a scornful name, haughtily ordered him to be silent, and finally marched out of his presence, declaring she would not re-enter it until he could finally drop all allusion to the subject.

With a half curse on his lips—he, so temperate and sweet-tempered a man!—Mr. Grubb went straight to Newgate, and obtained an interview with the prisoner. It came to nothing satisfactory; Charles was harder in his obstinacy than ever. From thence Mr. Grubb drove back to the West End, to Chenevix House. Some morning visitors were there, and Lady Mary Cleveland was exhibiting her baby to them. Mr. Grubb admired with the rest, and then made a sign to Grace. She followed him into the next room.

"I don't see what is to be done," he began. "Adela will not hear a word, will not admit anything, and I can make nothing of Charles Cleveland. Upon my mentioning Adela—of course, only in hints; I could not accuse my wife outright to him—he interrupted me with a request that I would not introduce Lady Adela's name into so painful a matter; that he had brought the disgrace upon himself, and was prepared to pay for it.

I think he may have lent the two notes to Adela. It would be but one hundred pounds out of the five. I cannot believe, if my wife were guilty, that Cleveland would take the penalty upon himself. Transportation for life, or whatever the sentence incurred may be, is no light matter, Grace."

Grace shuddered. " Do not let him incur the risk of it."

" I would rather cut off my right hand than punish a man unjustly, were he my greatest enemy. But unless I can get at the truth of this matter, and find proof that your view of it is correct, I shall have no plea, to my partner, to my bankers, or to my own conscience, for hushing it up ; and the law must take its course."

" Alas! alas! " murmured Lady Grace.

" You seem to overlook my feelings in this affair, Grace," he whispered, a deep hue dyeing his cheeks. " That she may have had something to do with it her paying away the notes proves : and to find the wife of your bosom thus in league with another —— You don't know what it is, Grace."

"I can imagine it," she answered, the tears standing in her eyes as she rose to answer his adieu. "Believe me, you have, and always have had, my deepest and truest sympathy; but Adela is my sister; what more can I say?"

Grace sat on, alone. The murmur of voices came to her from the adjacent room, but she heeded it not. She leaned her head upon her hand, and debated with herself. It was imperative that the real facts of the case should be brought to light; for if Charles Cleveland were permitted to stand his trial, perhaps to suffer the penalty of transportation, and it came out, later, that he was innocent, and her sister the guilty party, what a fearful position would be that of Adela!

Could Charley not be brought to confess through stratagem, mentally debated Grace. Suppose he were led to believe that Adela, to save him, had declared the truth, *then* he might speak. It was surely a good idea. Grace weighed it, in all its bearings, and thought the end would justify the means.

But to whom entrust so delicate a mission?
Not to Mr. Cleveland, he would betray it all
to Charles at the first sentence; not to Mr.
Grubb, his high sense of honour would never
let him intimate that Adela had confessed
what she had not; not to Lady Mary, for her
only idea of Newgate was that it was a place
overflowing with infectious fevers, which
she should inevitably bring home to baby.
Lord Acorn? Somehow Grace could not ask
him. Who next? Who else was there?
Herself? Yes, and Grace felt that none were
more fitted for the task than she was—she
who had the subject so much at heart. And
she resolved to go.

But she could not go alone to Newgate.
Her mother ought to be with her. Now the
matter, relative to the tracing of the notes to
Adela, had been kept from Lady Acorn.
Grace disclosed it to her in the emergency,
and made her the confidante of what she
meant to do.

Lady Acorn sat aghast. For once in her
life she was terrified to silence and meekness.
Grace obtained her consent, and the time for

the expedition was fixed. Not that Lady Acorn relished it.

"If it be as you and your father believe, Grace, Master Charley Cleveland deserves the soundest shaking man ever had yet," cried she, when speech returned to her.

"Ah, mamma! Then what must Adela deserve?"

"To be in Newgate herself," tartly responded Lady Acorn.

CHAPTER X.

A DISAGREEABLE EXPEDITION.

IT was Monday morning. Charles Cleveland sat on his iron bedstead in his dreary cell in Newgate: of which cell he had become heartily tired by this time: chewing there in solitude the cud of his reflections, which came crowding one upon another. None of them were agreeable, as may be imagined, but pressing itself upon him more keenly than all, was the sensation of deep, dark disappointment. Above the discomfort of his present position, above the sense of shame endured, above the hard, degrading life that loomed for him in the future, he felt the neglect of Lady Adela. She, for whom he was bearing all the misery and disgrace in this dreadful dungeon, had never, by letter or by message, sought to convey a ray of sympathy to cheer him. The neglect, the indifference may have been unavoidable, but it told not the less bitterly on the spirit of the prisoner.

A noise at his cell door. The heavy key was turning in the lock, and the prisoner looked up eagerly—a visit was such a break in his dreary day. Two ladies were entering, and his heart beat wildly—wildly ; for in the appearance of one he discerned some resemblance to Lady Adela's. *Had* she come to see him ! and he had been so ungratefully blaming her ! But the lady raised her veil, and he was re-called to his sober senses. It was only Grace Chenevix.

" So, Charles, an awful scrape you have brought yourself into, through your flirting nonsense with Adela ! " began the Countess of Acorn, as she followed her daughter in.

" Now, mamma, dear mamma," implored Grace, in a whisper, " if you interfere, you will ruin all."

" Ruin all ! much obliged to you, Grace ! I think he has ruined himself," retorted the Countess, in a shrill tone. Never famous for a sweet temper or a silent tongue, Lady Acorn was not improved by the trouble that had

fallen on them, or by this distasteful expedition which she had been forced, so to say,
to make this morning, for she could not allow
Grace to come alone. The unhappy prisoner
would reap the full benefit of her acrimony.

"I wonder you can look us in the face," she
went on to him. "Had anyone told me I
should some time walk through Newgate at-
tended by turnkeys, I should have said it was
a libel. We came down in a hack cab. I'd not
have brought the servants here for the world."

"I shall ever feel grateful to you," breathed
Charles."

"Oh, never mind about gratitude," unceremoniously interrupted Lady Acorn; "there's
no time for it. Let us say what we have to
say, Grace, and be gone. I'm all in a tremor,
lest those men with keys should come and
lock me up. Of course, Charles, you know it
has all come out."

Charles looked up sharply.

"Which is more luck than you could have
expected," added the Countess, while Grace
sat on thorns, lest some unlucky admission of
her mother's should ruin all, as she had

just phrased it, and unable to get a word
in edgeways. "Of all brainless simpletons
you are the worst. If Adela chose (like
the thoughtless, wicked girl she is, though
she is my daughter) to write her husband's
name to a cheque, was that any reason why
you should go hotheaded to work, and make
believe you did it? Mr. Grubb is not your
husband, and you have no right to his money:
Things that the law will permit a wife to do
with impunity, you might be run up to the
drop for."

"Who has been saying this?" breathed
the prisoner, bewildered with the torrent of
words, and their signification. "Surely not
Lady Adela."

"Charles," interposed Grace, and her quiet
tones, after those of the Countess, sounded
like the lulling of a storm, "there is no
necessity for further mystery, or for your continuing to assume the guilt; which, as my
mother says, was an unwise step on your
part ——"

"I did not say unwise," sharply interrupted
the Countess; "call things by their right

names, Lady Grace. It was insanity, and nobody but an idiot would have done it. That's what I said."

"The circumstances are known to us now," went on Grace, speaking quietly. "Poor Adela, at her wits' end for money, drew the cheque, and sent you to cash it. And then, terrified at what she had done, persuaded you to assume the responsibilty."

"She did not persuade me," explained Charles, falling completely into the snare, and believing every word that was spoken, yet still anxious to excuse Lady Adela. "I volunteered to bear it. And I would do as much again."

"Charles—mamma, pray let me speak for a minute—had you been present when Adela wrote the cheque, you would have been doubly to blame. She——"

Charles shook his head. "I was not present."

"She, poor thing, was excited at the moment, and incapable of reflection, but you ought to have recalled her to reason, and refused to aid in it—for her own sake."

"And of course I should," eagerly answered Mr. Charles, "had I known there was anything wrong about it. She brought me the cheque, ready filled in ———"

"When you went up from the City for the cheque-book, on the Saturday morning. Yes, we know all."

"I declare I thought it was Mr. Grubb's writing, if ever I saw his writing in my life. I was not likely to have any other thought—how could I have? And I never recalled the matter to my mind, or knew anything more about it, till the Monday night, when I came up from Netherleigh : as I suppose Lady Adela has told you, if she has told you the rest."

"And then you undertook to shield her," interposed Lady Acorn, "and a glorious mess you have made of it between you. Grace, how you worry! you can speak when I have done. What *she* did would have been hushed up by her husband for all our sakes, but what you did was a very different matter. And the disgrace you have gratuitously brought upon yourself may yet be blazoned forth to every corner of the United Kingdom."

"And these are all the thanks I get," remarked Charles, striving to speak lightly.

"What other thanks would you like?" retorted the Countess. "A service of plate presented to you? You deserve a testimonial, don't you, to have run your head into a noose of this dangerous kind for any woman! And for Adela, of all others, who cares for nobody on earth but her blessed self. Not she."

"My mother is right," said Lady Grace, "and it may be as well, Charles, that you should know it. Adela has never cared for you in any way, save as an amusing boy, who could talk nonsense to her when she chose to condescend to listen. If you have thought anything else ——"

"I never had a disloyal thought to Lady Adela," interrupted Charles, warmly. "Or to her husband—who has always been so kind to me. I would have warded all such—all ill—from her with my life."

"And nicely she has repaid you!" commented Lady Acorn. "Do you suppose she would have confessed this herself?—no, we found it out. She would have let you suffer,

and never said ' Thank you.'   *I* tell you this,
Master Charley ; and I hope you will let it
prove to you what the smiles of a heartless
butterfly of a married woman are worth."

He bit his dry and fevered lips with mortification—fevered for *her*.   And Lady Acorn,
after bestowing a few more unpalatable truths
upon the unhappy prisoner, took her daughter's arm and hurried away, glad to escape
from the place and the interview.

" A capital success we have had, Gracie,"
she cried, when they had got outside the
stone walls, " but it's all thanks to me.   You
would have beat about the bush, and palavered,
and hesitated, and done no good. I got it out
of him nicely—like the green sea-gull that the
boy is.   But, Grace, my child "—and Lady
Acorn's voice for once grew hushed and
solemn—" what in the world will be done
with Adela ? "

It was a painful scene, that in which they
brought it home to Lady Adela. When Lady
Acorn carried to her husband the news of
Charles's unconscious avowal, he was struck

almost dumb with consternation. The worst
conclusion he had come to, in regard to some
of the notes being traced to his daughter,
was that she had but borrowed money from
Charles Cleveland.　Innocently.　Yes; he
could not and would not think she had any
knowledge of how Charles became possessed
of the notes.　Lord Acorn, in spite of his
perpetual embarrassments, and his not altogether straightforward shifts to evade them,
possessed the true sense of honour that generally pertains to his order.　He possessed it
especially in regard to woman; and to find
that his most favoured and favourite daughter
had been guilty of theft; of—of—he could
not pursue the thought, he sank down with
his pain.

"We had better go to her, and hear what
she has to plead in excuse, and—and—ascer-
tain how far her peculations have gone," he
said presently to his wife.　"Perhaps there are
more of them.　Poor Grubb!"

So they went to Grosvenor Square, arm-
in-arm, but sick at heart, and found Lady
Adela alone.　She was toying with a golden

bird in a golden cage ; gold at any rate in
colour ; a recent purchase. Her afternoon
dress of muslin had golden-hued sprigs upon
it, and there was much gilding of mirrors
and other ornaments in the room, the taste of
that day. A gay scene altogether, and Adela
the gayest and prettiest object in it.

She was not quite as heartless, though, as
appeared on the surface, or as Lady Acorn
judged her to be. Adela was growing frightened.
She was beginning to realise what it was she
had done, and to wonder, in much self-tor-
ment, what would come of it. That Mr.
Grubb would release Charles Cleveland she
had not at first entertained the smallest doubt,
or that the affair would be entirely hushed up.
Charles would be true to her, never disclose
her name, and there it would end. With this
fond expectation she had buoyed herself up ;
but as the days went on, and Charles was
still kept in Newgate, soon to be brought
up for another examination preparatory to
committal for trial, she grew alarmed. For
the past day or two her uneasiness had been
intolerable. Could she have saved Charles

and his good name by confessing the truth, and run away for ever from the sight of men, she would have done it thankfully; but to take the guilt upon herself, and such debasing guilt, *and* remain before the world!—this was utterly repugnant, not to say impossible, to the proud heart of Lady Adela.

It was so unusual to see her father and mother come in together, and to see them both with solemn faces, that Adela's heart leaped, as the saying runs, into her mouth. Still, it *might* not portend any adverse meaning, and she rallied her courage.

"I want to make him sing," she cried, turning on them her bright and smiling face. "Did you ever see so beautiful a colour, papa? I *hope* he is not too beautiful to sing."

But there was no answering smile on the faces of either father or mother, only an increased solemnity. Lord Acorn, waving his hand towards the bird as if he would wave off a too frivolous toy, touched her arm and pointed to a chair.

"Sit down, Adela."

She turned as white as death. Lady Acorn

opened her lips to begin, a great wrath evidently upon them, but her lord and master
imperatively waved his hand to her for silence,
as he had just waved away the frivolous bird,
and addressed his daughter.

"What is to become of you, Adela?"

She neither spoke nor moved. She sat
back in an arm-chair, with her white and
terror-stricken face. Her teeth began to
chatter.

"How came you to do it?" he continued.

"To—to—do what?" she gasped.

"To do what!" screamed out Lady Acorn,
utterly unable to control her tongue and her
reproaches longer—"why, to rifle your husband's cheque-book of a cheque, and fill it in,
and forge the firm's signature, and despatch
that unsuspicious baby, Charles Cleveland, to
cash it."

"Who—who says I did that?" asked
Adela, making one last, hopeless, desperate
effort to defend herself.

"Who ——"

"Betsy, if you can't let me speak, you had
better go away for a few minutes," cried Lord

Acorn, arresting a fresh burst of eloquence from his wife. "That you did do this thing, Adela, is known now; some of the notes have been traced to you, all the particulars have been traced, and Charles Cleveland has confessed to them. Any denial you could attempt would be more idle than the chirping of that bird."

"Charles has confessed to them?" she whispered, taken aback by this blow. Nothing, save his confession, could have brought it absolutely home to her.

"Did you set up a fantastic hope that he would keep silence to the end, and go to his hanging to save you?" demanded Lady Acorn, defying her lord's wish to have the whole ball to himself. "Proofs came out against you, Madam Adela, as your father says; they were carried to Charles Cleveland, and he could but admit the truth."

"*Why* did you do this terrible thing?— That my daughter, whom I have so loved, should be capable of sullying herself with such disgrace!" broke off Lord Acorn, with a wail. In good truth, it had been a blow to him, and one he had never bargained for. To play a little at Lady Sanely's for amusement, was one thing; he had, so to say, winked at that; but to *gamble* and to steal money to pay her gambling debts, was quite another. "Adela, I could almost wish I had died before hearing of it."

Adela burst into tears. "I wanted the money so badly," she sobbed, hiding her face with her trembling hands. "I owed it—a great deal—to people at Lady Sanely's. I was at my wits' end, and Mr. Grubb would not give me any more. Oh, papa, forgive me! Can't it be hushed up?"

"Did you help yourself to more than that?" asked Lord Acorn.

"I do not understand," she faltered, not catching his meaning.

"Have you drawn or used any other false cheque?"

"Oh, no, no; only that. Papa, *won't* you forgive me?"

He shook his head. No, he felt that he could not. "My forgiveness may not be of vital consequence to you, one way or the other, Adela," he remarked with a groan, that he drowned by coughing. "The termination of this affair does not lie with me."

"It lies with my husband," she said, in a low tone. "He will hush it up."

"It does not lie with him, Adela," sternly spoke Lord Acorn. "Had it been one of his private cheques, had you used his name only, it might in a great degree have rested with him—unless the bankers had taken it up."

"But you borrowed old Mr. Howard's name as well," struck in Lady Acorn; "and, if he pleases to be stern and obstinate, he can just place you where Charles Cleveland is, and you would have to stand your trial in the face and eyes of the world. A pretty disgrace for us all! A frightful calamity."

Adela looked from one to the other, her face changing pitiably; now white as snow with fear, now hectic with emotion and shame.

"Mr. Grubb has full power in Leadenhall Street," she pleaded. "He will take care to shield *me*."

"Are you sure of that?" quietly asked her father. "Has your conduct to him been such—I don't allude to this one pitiable instance, I speak of your treatment of him generally—has it been such that you can assume he will inevitably go out of his way to shield you, right or wrong?"

In spite of the miserable shame that filled her, a passing flush of triumph crossed her face. Ay! and her heart. What though she *had* persistently done her best to estrange her husband, with her provoking ways and her scornful contumely, very conscious felt she that she was all in all to him still. Why, had he not begged of her to confide this thing to him, and he would make it straight and guard her from exposure?

"I have nothing to fear from him, papa; I know it. It will be all right."

"How can you assert this in barefaced confidence, you wicked child!" groaned Lady Acorn. "I'd not—no, I'd not be so brazen for the world."

"Adela, don't deceive yourself with vain expectations; it may be harder for you in the end," interposed her father, once more making a deprecatory motion towards the place where his wife's tongue lay. "You are assuming a surety which you have no right to feel; better look the truth sternly in the face."

"I am his wife, papa," she faintly urged. "He will be *sure* to shelter me."

"He may be able to shelter you from exposure; I doubt not but that he will do it, so far as he can, for his own sake as well as for yours; for all our sakes, indeed. But ——"

"A few years ago you might have been hanged," struck in Lady Acorn. "Hanged outside Newgate. I can remember the time when death was the penalty for forgery. Dr. Dodd was hung for it. How would you have liked that."

Adela did not say how she would have liked it. She was passing her hands nervously across her face, as if to keep down its pallor. As to Lord Acorn, he despaired of being allowed to finish any argument he might begin, and paced the room restlessly.

"But, though your husband may shield you from public exposure, it is too much to hope that he will absolve you from consequences, and I think you will have to face and bear them," recommenced Lord Acorn, talking while he walked. "Had my wife served me as you have served Grubb, I should have put her away from me for ever; and I tell it you, Adela, before her as she stands there, though she is your mother."

"And served me right, too," commented Lady Acorn.

"How do you mean, papa?" gasped Adela.

"My meaning ought to be plain enough," was Lord Acorn's angry reproof. "Are you wilfully shutting your eyes to the nature of the offence you have sullied yourself with?— its degradation?—its sin?" he sharply questioned. "There's hardly a worse in our criminal code, that I know of, except murder."

"But I do not understand," she faintly reiterated. "If my husband absolves me, who else ——"

"He may absolve you so far as the general public goes, shield you from that penalty," was the impatient interruption; "but not from your offence to himself. In my judgment you must not look for that."

Adela did not answer. She glanced at

her father questioningly, with an imploring look.

"A man has put his wife away from him for a much less cause than this," continued Lord Acorn. "And your husband, I fancy, must have been already pretty nigh tired out. What has your conduct been to him, Adela, ever since your marriage?"

She bent her head, her face flushing. To be taken to task by her father was a bitter pill, in addition to all the other discomfort.

"*It has been shameful!*" emphatically pronounced Lord Acorn. "For my part, I marvel that Grubb has borne it. But that I make it a rule not to interfere with my daughters, once they have left my roof for that of a husband, I should not have borne it tamely for him; and that I now tell you, Adela. One or two hints that I have given you from time to time you have disregarded."

"He has borne with her and indulged her to the top of her bent, when he ought to have taken her by the shoulders and shaken her insolence out of her," nodded the mother.

"Had you been a loving wife, Adela, things

might have a better chance of going well with you," pursued her father, with another motion of the hand. " But, remembering what your treatment of your husband has persistently been, you can have no plea for praying leniency of him now, or he much inclination to accord it."

Lady Adela would have liked to give her head a saucy toss. She knew better; her father could not judge of her husband as she could. " Francis can't beat me," she thought. " He can lecture me, and *will*; and I must bear it meekly for once, under the circumstances."

She looked up at her father.

" My husband is very fond of me, in spite of all," she whispered.

" Yes, he is fond of you," returned Lord Acorn, with emotion. " Too fond. His behaviour to you proves that. Why, how much money have you had of him, drawn from him by your wiles, beyond your large legitimate allowance ? "

Adela did not answer. " Has he spoken of it ? " she asked, the question occurring to her.

"No, he has not spoken of it; he is not the man to speak of it. I gather so much from your sisters : they talk of it amid themselves. One might have thought that your husband's generous kindness to you would have won your regard, had nothing else done it. It strikes me all that will be over now," concluded Lord Acorn.

Adela answered by a sobbing sigh.

"You have been on the wrong tack for some time now," he resumed, as an afterthought. "Who but a silly-minded woman would have made herself ridiculous, as you have, by flirting with a boy like Charles Cleveland ? Do ——"

"Oh, papa! You cannot think for a moment I meant anything !" she exclaimed, her cheeks flushing hotly.

"Except to vex your husband. Do you think your foolishness—I could call it by a harsher name—did not give sorrow to myself and your mother ? We had deemed you sensible, honourable, open as the day : not the hard-hearted, frivolous woman you have turned out to be. Well, Adela, people generally have to reap what they sow; and I fear your harvest will not be a pleasant one."

She pressed her trembling hands together.

"Where are you going?" inquired Lady Acorn, as her husband took his hat up.

"To Leadenhall Street—to Grubb. *Some* one must apprise him of this dreadful truth; and I suppose it falls to me to do it—and a most distressing task it is. Would you have allowed young Cleveland to stand his trial? —to have suffered the penalty of the crime?" broke off Lord Acorn to his daughter.

"It would never have come to that, papa."

"But it would have come to it; it was coming to it. I ask, would you have allowed an innocent lad to be sent over the seas for you?"

Adela shuddered. "I must have spoken then," was her faint answer.

Lord Acorn, jumping into a cab, proceeded to Leadenhall Street, to make this wretched confession to his son-in-law. Had he been making it of himself, he would have felt it less. He was, however, spared the task. Mr. Grubb was not in the City, and Mr. Grubb already knew the truth.

It chanced that, close upon the departure of Lady Acorn and her daughter Grace from Charles Cleveland's cell that morning, Serjeant Mowham was shown into it : and the reader may as well be reminded that the learned Serjeant had not taken up Charles's case in his professional capacity, but simply as an anxious friend. Without going into details, Charles told him that the truth had now come out, his innocence was made apparent to those concerned, and he hoped he should soon see the last of the precious walls he was incarcerated in. Away rushed Serjeant Mowham to Leadenhall Street, asking an explanation of Messrs. Grubb and Howard ; and very much surprised did he feel at finding those gentlemen knew nothing.

"I am positive it is a fact," persisted the Serjeant to them. "One cannot mistake Charley's changed tones and looks. Some evidence that exculpates him has turned up, rely upon it, and I thought, of course, you must know what it was. Lady Acorn and one of her daughters went out from him just before I got there."

Mr. Grubb felt curious; rather uneasy. If Charles Cleveland was exonerated, who had been the culprit?

"I shall go and see him at once," he said to Mr. Howard.

And now Charles Cleveland fell into another error. Never supposing but that Mr. Grubb must know at least as much as Lady Acorn knew, he unconsciously betrayed all. In his eagerness to show his kind patron he was not quite the ungrateful wretch he appeared to be, he betrayed it.

"I never thought of such a thing, sir, as that it was not your cheque—I mean your own signature," he pleaded. "I'd not have done such a thing for all the world—and after all your goodness to me for so many months! It was only when I came up from Netherleigh on the Monday evening I found there was something wrong with it."

"You heard it from Lady Adela," spoke Mr. Grubb, quietly accepting the mistake.

"Yes. She told me how it was. Mr. Howard was with you then in the dining-room, and his coming had frightened her.

She seemed in dreadful distress, and I promised to shield her as far as I could ———"

"You should have confided the truth to me," interrupted Mr. Grubb. "All trouble might have been avoided."

"But how could I?—and after my voluntary promise! What would you have thought of me, sir, had I shifted the blame from myself to lay it upon her?" added Charley, lifting his ingenuous, honest eyes to his master's.

Mr. Grubb did not say what he should have thought. Charles rather misinterpreted the silence: he fancied Mr. Grubb must be angry with him.

"Of course it has been a heavy blow to me, the being accused of such a thing, and to have had to accept the accusation, and to lie here in Newgate, with no prospect before me but transportation; but I ask you what else I could do, sir? I could not clear myself at the expense of Lady Adela."

Mr. Grubb did not answer this appeal. Telling Charles that steps should be taken for his release, and enjoining him to absolute silence as regarded Lady Adela's name, he returned to Leadenhall Street, and held a private conference with his partner.

What passed at it was known only to themselves, or how far Francis Grubb found it necessary to speak of his wife. Mr. Howard noticed one thing—that the young man (young, as compared with himself) looked at moments utterly bewildered; once or twice he talked at random. The following morning was the one fixed for Charles's second examination before Sir Turtle Kite, when, that worthy alderman being satisfied, he must of course be released.

Barely was the conference over and this resolution fixed upon, when a most urgent summons came to Mr. Grubb from Blackheath —his mother was supposed to be dying. He started off without the loss of a moment. And when, some time later, the Earl of Acorn arrived, he found only Mr. Howard, and learnt from him that Charles would be discharged on the following morning.

Just for a moment we must return to Adela. When Lady Acorn left her—after exhausting her whole vocabulary in the art of scolding, and waiting to drink some tea she asked for, for her lips were dry—Adela buried her face on the gold-coloured satin sofa cushion, and indulged her repentance to her heart's content. It was sincere—and bitter. Were the time to come over again—oh, that it could! —far rather would she cut off her right hand than do what she had done; she would die, rather than do such a thing again. It was altogether a dreadful prospect yet—at least, it might be. What if they would not exonerate Charley without inculpating her? Not her husband; she did not fear him; old Howard, and the bankers, and those aldermen on the bench? How should she meet it? where should she run to? what would the world say of her? Lady Adela started from the cushion affrighted. Her lips were more parched than her mother's had been, and she rang for some tea on her own score.

She sat back in her chair after drinking it, her pretty hands lying listless on her pretty dress, and tried to think matters out. As soon as her husband came home she would throw herself upon his bosom and confess all, and plead for mercy with tears and kisses as she had never pleaded before, and give him her word never to touch another card, and whisper that in future she would be his dear wife. He would not refuse to forgive her; no fear of that; he would tell her not to be naughty again, and make all things right. She would tell him that she might have loved him from the first, for it was the truth, but that she steeled her heart and her temper against him, because of his name and of his being a City man; and she would tell him that she could and should love him from henceforth, that the past was past, and they would be as happy together as the day was long.

A yearning impatience grew upon her for his return as she sat and thought thus. What hour was it? Surely he was at home sometimes earlier than this!

As she turned her head to look at the timepiece on the marble console, Hilson came in, a note on his small silver salver.

"One of the clerks brought it up from Leadenhall Street, my lady," he remarked, as

he held it out to her. "He said there was
no answer."

It was not her husband's writing, and Lady
Adela opened it with trembling fingers. Had
some new and dreadful phase turned up in
this unhappy business? The fear, that it
had, flashed through her.

"DEAR MADAM,—Mr. Grubb has been sent
for to his mother, who is dangerously ill. He
requested me to drop you a line to say he
should probably remain at Blackheath for the
night. I therefore do so, and despatch it to
you by a clerk.

" Your obedient servant,

" JAMES HOWARD."

·" So I can't do it," she cried, thinking of
all she had been planning out, something like
resentment making itself heard in her dis-
appointed heart. " What a wretched evening it will be !"

Wretched enough. She did not venture
to go to Chenevix House while lying under
its wrathful displeasure; she had not the face

to show herself elsewhere in this uncertainty and trouble.

" I wish," she burst forth, with a petulant tap of her black satin slipper on the carpet, " I wish that tiresome Mrs. Lynn would get well ! Or else die, and have done with it."

The Lady Adela was not altogether in an entirely penitential frame of mind yet.

CHAPTER XI.

SIR TURTLE KITE.

WHAT a delightful world this might be if all our fond plans and hopes could but be fulfilled! if no adverse influence crept in to frustrate them!

Never a doubt had crossed the mind of those concerned for the welfare of Charles Cleveland, that he would be set at liberty on Tuesday, the day following the one above spoken of.

It was not to be. Charles was brought up, as previously, for private examination before Alderman Sir Turtle Kite. No evidence was offered; on the contrary, a legal gentleman, one Mr. Primerly, the noted solicitor for the house of Grubb and Howard, intimated that there was none to offer—the charge had been a mistake altogether.

Sir Turtle Kite was a little man, as broad

as he was long, with a smiling round face and
shiny bald head, the best-hearted, easiest-
natured, and pleasantest-tempered of all the
bench of aldermen. He would fain have
been lenient to the worst offender ; added to
which, he knew about as much of the law as
he did of the new comet, just then spreading
its tail in the heavens. Therefore, unconsciously lacking the acumen to make an able
administrator of justice, Sir Turtle, as a natural sequence, was especially fond of sitting
to administer it. Latterly he had sat daily,
and generally alone, much gout and dyspepsia
prevailing just then amidst his brother aldermen. The Lord Mayor of the year was a
bon vivant, and gave a civic dinner five days
in the week. Certain recent judicial deci-
sions of Sir Turtle's, mild as usual, had been
called in question by the newspapers; and
one of them sharply attacked him in a lead-
ing article, asking why he did not discharge
every prisoner brought before him, and regale
him with luncheon.

Reading this article at breakfast, Sir Turtle
came forth to the magisterial bench this day,

Tuesday, smarting under its castigation. And, to the utter surprise of everyone in the private justice room, he declined to release the prisoner, Charles Cleveland. Rubbing his bald head, and making the best little speech he could—he was no orator—Sir Turtle talked of the fatal effects that might arise from the miscarriage of justice, and his resolve to uphold it in all its integrity.

Mr. Grubb was not present. Mr. Howard, who was, stared with astonishment, having always known the benevolent little alderman to be as pliant as a bit of cap-paper. James Howard said what he dared; as much as it was expedient to say, against the alderman's decision; but to no purpose. Sir Turtle, trying to put the wisdom of an owl into his round face, demanded to know, if the prisoner was not guilty, who was? This not being satisfactorily explained, he remanded the prisoner to the following morning, when he would probably be committed for trial. And, with this consolatory decision, Charles was conveyed back to his lodgings in Newgate.

Mr. Howard, somewhat put out by the

contretemps, and by the alderman's rejection of his declared testimony that the prisoner was innocent, wrote a note to Lord Acorn with the news, and sent it to Chenevix House by hand. He had promised to notify the release of Charles, when that should be accomplished. But he had to notify a very different fact.

"Bless my heart!" exclaimed Lord Acorn, when he opened the note late in the afternoon, for he (also relieved of his worst fears) had been out gadding. "This is a dreadful thing!"

"What is the matter?" cried his wife, who was sitting there with Grace. "One would think the world was coming to an end to look at your face."

The Earl's face just then was considerably lengthened. He stood twirling his whiskers, and gazing at James Howard's very plain handwriting.

"They won't release Cleveland, Howard writes me," said the Earl. "Things have taken a cross turn."

Grace closed her book and clasped her

hands. Lady Acorn threw down her knitting, and inquired who would not release him?

"The magistrate who has sat to hear the case," replied Lord Acorn. "Sir—what's the odd name?—Turtle Kite. He refuses, absolutely, to release Charles, until the true culprit shall be brought before him— seems to think it is a trick, Howard says."

"Good heavens!" cried Lady Grace, fore-seeing more dire consequences than she would have liked to speak of. "What will become of Charles? What of Adela? Oh, papa! they cannot compel her to appear, can they? ——to take Charles's place?"

"I don't know what they can do," gloomily responded the Earl. "Hang these aldermen! What right have they to turn obstinate, when a prisoner's innocency is vouched for?"

"And where *is* the prisoner?" cried my lady.

"Taken back to Newgate. Is to be brought up again to-morrow, *to be committed for trial.* Well, this is a pretty kettle of fish!"

Grace bit her pale and trembling lips. "Was Mr. Grubb at the examination, papa?"

"No. Grubb's at Blackheath. Has not been up, Howard says, since he went down yesterday. What on earth is to be done?"

"The best thing to do is for you to go to Blackheath and see Mr. Grubb," promptly cried the Countess. "If Adela were a child, I should beat her. Bringing all this worry and disgrace upon us!"

"I couldn't go there and be back for the dinner," cried he. For they were engaged that evening to a state dinner at a duke's.

"Bother dinner!" irascibly retorted Lady Acorn. "If this affair can't be stopped, Adela will have to be smuggled over to the Continent, and stay in hiding there. If it is *not* stopped, and her name has to appear, we shall never be able to show our faces at a dinner-table again."

Lord Acorn passed his hand over his perplexed brow. Look at the affair in what way they would, it seemed to present nothing but difficulty. Once Charles Cleveland was committed for trial, what would be the end of it? He *could not* be allowed to stand his trial— and what might not that involve for Adela?

Lord Acorn, hating personal trouble of all kinds, especially trouble so disagreeable as this, betook himself—not to Blackheath, as enjoined by his wife, but to the City. He would see Mr. Howard first, and hear what his opinion was. Jumping out of the cab which had conveyed him to Leadenhall Street, he jumped against Serjeant Mowham.

"No good your going up," cried the Serjeant. "Howard has left, and Grubb seems to be nowhere to-day."

"Have you heard about poor Charley?" asked Lord Acorn.

"Of course I have; that has brought me here. Primerly came to my chambers on other business, and told me what had happened. I came down here at once to catch one of the partners—or both of them—and see if there's anything to be done."

"What can be done?" returned Lord Acorn.

"Be shot if I know," said the Serjeant. "It will be a serious thing for Charley, mind you, if he does get committed for trial—as Sir Turtle Kite has promised."

" What an ill-conditioned, revengeful man that Sir Turtle Kite must be ! "

" There you are wrong, my lord. He is just the contrary : one of the sunniest-natured little men you can picture, and about as able upon the bench as my old wig would be if you stuck it there. The newspapers have been going in to him lately for his leniency, so I suppose he thinks he must make an example of somebody. One of the papers had a bantering article this morning, suggesting that Sir Turtle should open a luncheon room at the court, and treat the delinquents who appeared before him to bottled stout and oysters. That article, I suspect, is the cause of his turning crusty to-day. Look here," added the Serjeant, lowering his voice and catching hold of the other's botton-hole, " what is there at the bottom of all this matter ? Who was it that Charley made himself a scapegoat for ? Do you know ? "

As it chanced, they were jostled just then by some one of the many passers-by in the busy street—nearly pushed off the causeway. Lord Acorn, forgetting his usual superlative equanimity, allowed himself to be put out by it, and so evaded an answer.

"Nobody does know, that I can find out," said the Serjeant, returning to the charge, and facing Lord Acorn, with whom he had long been on intimate terms: "and Charley makes a mystery of it. I suspect it was some one of those wild blades he has been hand-in-glove with lately—and that he won't betray him."

"Ah, yes, no doubt," carelessly assented Lord Acorn, his face wearing a deeper tinge than ordinary. "I wonder where Howard is? Charley must be saved."

"It will be of no use your seeing Howard, Lord Acorn—except for any odds and ends of information he might afford you. The affair is out of his hands now."

"But it can't be out of Mr. Grubb's!"

"Indeed it is. It is in Sir Turtle Kite's."

"Could one do any good with *him*?"

Serjeant Mowham laughed. "I can't say, one way or the other. You might try, perhaps. Don't say, though, that I recommended it."

The peer smoothed his brow, smooth

enough before to all appearance. How often do these smiling brows hide a heavy load of perplexity within!

"As for me, I must be off," added the Serjeant. "I've a consultation on for five o'clock, at my chambers, and I believe five has struck."

He bustled away, leaving Lord Acorn in the crowd. Thought is quick. That nobleman was saying to himself, "What if I *do* see Sir Turtle?——who knows but I might come over him by persuasion? Wonder where he is to be found?"

He glanced up and down Leadenhall Street, at its houses on this side and on that, as if, haply, he might discern the name. During this survey he found himself subjected to an increased amount of jostling, and became aware that the clerks were pouring out of the offices of Grubb and Howard.

"Oh—ah," began Lord Acorn, addressing a young man who was nearly the last, all his nonchalance of manner in full force again, " can you tell me where Sir Turtle Kite is to be found?"

"Sir Turtle Kite, sir?" replied the young clerk civilly. "I think—I'm not quite sure —but I think his place is somewhere down by the river. Here—Aitcheson"—stopping an older clerk—"where is Sir Turtle Kite's place? This gentleman is asking."

"Tooley Street — forget the number— can't mistake it," replied the other, who seemed in a vast hurry to get away, and threw back the words as he went.

"Tooley Street," repeated Lord Acorn aloud, by way of impressing the name on his mind. "Some commercial stronghold, I apprehend. What business is he?"

"He's a tallow merchant, sir."

"Ah—thank you — a tallow merchant," repeated his lordship, with a deprecatory shrug of the shoulders at the objectionable word, tallow. "Thank you very much." And the young man, who was of good breeding, lifted his hat and walked away.

Lord Acorn had as much notion in which direction he must look for Tooley Street as he might have had in looking for the way to the North Pole. Making another inquiry, this

time of a policeman, the road was pointed
out to him, and the information given that it
was "not far." That, at least, was the
policeman's opinion.

So Lord Acorn, whose cab had been dismissed at first, and who liked walking, for
he was a lithe, active man for his age, at
length reached Tooley Street, and began a
pilgrimage up and down its narrow confines,
which seemed to be choked up with cumber-
some drays and trolleys. Presently he discovered a huge pile of dark buildings, all
along the wide face of which was posted the
name of the firm: "Turtle Kite, Tanner,
Rex, and Co." The goal at last!

Wondering within himself how Sir Turtle
Kite, or any other person possessing rational
instincts and ordinary lungs, could exist in
such an atmosphere of dirt and turmoil, Lord
Acorn looked about for the entrance. There
was none to be seen: and he was beginning
seriously to speculate whether Turtle Kite,
Tanner, Rex, and Co. entered the building by
means of a rope ladder affixed to one of the
little square holes that served for windows,

when a man, who had the appearance of a porter, came out of a narrow, dark entry.

"Is there any entrance to this building, my man?"

"Entrance is up here, sir; waggon entrance on t'other side."

"Oh—ah—you belong to it, I perceive. Do you happen to know whether Sir Turtle Kite is in?"

"There's nobody in at all, sir; warehouses is shut for the evening," returned the porter. "Sir Turtle don't come here much hisself now; he leaves things mostly to Tanner and Rex. They'll both be here to-morrow morning, sir. Watchman's coming on presently."

"Ah, yes, no doubt," assented Lord Acorn in his suave way. "Then Sir Turtle does not live here, I presume."

The porter checked a laugh at the notion. "Sir Turtle lives at Brixton, sir. Leastways, it's between Brixton and Clapham. Rosemary Lodge, sir—a rare beautiful place it is."

Brixton now! To Lord Acorn's dismayed mind it seemed that he might almost as well start for the moon; and for a few seconds he hesitated. But—having undertaken this adventurous expedition—adventurous in more ways than one—he must carry it through for his unhappy daughter's sake.

" Do you fancy Sir Turtle is likely to be at home now, at—ah, Rosemary House—if I go there, my man ? "

" Most likely, sir. He is mostly at home earlier than this. Sir Turtle is very fond of his gardens and greenhouses, you see, and makes haste home to 'em. He's got no wife nor child. But it's Rosemary Lodge, sir ; not Rosemary House."

" Ah, yes, thank you—Rosemary Lodge," repeated his lordship, dropping a shilling into the porter's hand, and hailing the first cab he met.

" Rosemary Lodge, Brixton," said he to the driver.

" Yes, sir. What part of Brixton ? "

" Don't know at all," said his lordship: " Never was at Brixton in my life."

" Brixton's a straggling sort of place, you see, sir. I might be driving you about ——"

" It is between Brixton and Clapham,"

interrupted the Earl. "Rosemary Lodge: Sir Turtle Kite's."

"Oh come, the name's something," said the man, as he drove off.

Rosemary Lodge was not difficult to find, once the locality was reached. It was a large and very pretty white villa, painted glass borders surrounding its windows, and it stood in the midst of a spacious lawn dotted with beds of bright flowers. Walking round the gravel drive, Lord Acorn rang at the door, which was speedily opened by a man in chocolate-coloured livery.

"Is Sir Turtle Kite at home?"

"Yes, sir; but he is at dinner; just sat down to it."

"At dinner!" echoed Lord Acorn. "I want to see him very particularly."

"Well, sir, Sir Turtle does not much like to be disturbed at his dinner," hesitated the man. "Perhaps you could wait?—or call again?"

"Look here," said Lord Acorn, hunting in his pocket for his card-case, a bright idea seizing him, "you shall ask Sir Turtle to allow me to go into the dining-room to him, and I'll say the few words I have to say while he dines. I suppose he is alone! I won't disturb him from it. Hang it!" muttered his lordship, finding he had not his card-case with him. "You must take in my name: Lord Acorn."

This colloquy took place in the hall. At that moment another serving man came out of the dining-room—his master wanted to know what the stir was. Lord Acorn caught a glimpse of a well-spread table, and of a round good-humoured face above it. "Announce me," he rapidly said: and the servant did so.

"Lord Acorn."

Up rose Sir Turtle, his beaming countenance looking its surprise, his napkin tucked into his uppermost button-hole. Lord Acorn, a fascinating-mannered man as any living, entered upon his courtly apology, his short explanation, and offered his hand. In two minutes his lordship was seated at the dinner-table, regaling himself with real turtle soup, served out of a silver tureen; he and his host laughing and talking together as freely as though they were friends of years.

"It is so very good of you to ask me to partake of your dinner in this impromptu way, Sir Turtle," remarked his lordship. "I should have lost mine. We were to have dined—I and my wife—with the Duke of Dunford this evening, but I could not have got back for it. As to my business, the little matter I have come down to you to speak of, I won't trouble you with that until dinner's over."

"Quite right, my lord," said the Knight. "Never unite eating and business together when it can be avoided. As to your lordship's partaking of my dinner, such as it is, the obligation lies on my side, and I think it very condescending of you."

Sir Turtle Kite, knight, alderman, and tallow merchant, held the same reverence for dukes and lords that many another Sir Turtle holds, and his round face and his little bald head shone again with the honour of having the Earl of Acorn as a guest. But he need not have disparaged his dinner by saying "such as it is!" Lord Acorn had rarely sat down to a better. The Knight liked to dine well, and he had a rare good cook.

"As rich as Crœsus, I know; these city men always are," thought Lord Acorn. "And he is as genial a little man as one could wish to meet, and not objectionable in any way," mentally added his lordship as the dinner went on.

It was not until the wine was on the table, and the servants were gone, that Lord Acorn entered upon and explained the subject which had brought him. He spoke rather lightly, interspersing praises of the wines, which for goodness matched the dishes. One bottle of choice claret, brought up specially for his lordship to taste, was truly of rare quality.

"It would be so very dreadful a thing if this honest-minded, chivalrous young fellow were to be compelled to stand a trial," continued the Earl confidentially, as he sipped the claret. "Painful to your generous heart, I am quite sure, Sir Turtle, as well as to mine and Mr. Grubb's."

"Of course it would, my lord."

"And I thought I would come to you myself and privately explain. By allowing this young fellow to be released to-morrow, you will be doing a righteous and a generous act."

Sir Turtle nodded. "But what a young fool the lad must be to have allowed the world to think him guilty!" he remarked. "*Who* is it that he is screening, do you say, my lord? Some unfortunate acquaintance of his, who had got into a mess? Was the fellow also staying at Grubb's."

Lord Acorn coughed. "Yes; the culprit was staying in Grosvenor Square at the time. He, the true criminal, is out of the law's reach now, and can't be caught," added the Earl, drawing upon his invention: "And we wish to keep his name quiet, and give him another chance. But, that the prisoner who has been twice before you is innocent as the day, I give you my solemn word of honour. I hope you will release him, dear Sir Turtle."

"I will," assented Sir Turtle. "There's my hand upon it. And those libellous news-papers may go and be—hanged."

Perhaps the word hanged was not exactly the one Sir Turtle rapped out in his zeal. But he was not before his own magisterial bench just then. Lord Acorn clasped the hand warmly. He had taken quite a fancy to the genial little alderman, and he felt inexpressibly grateful.

"I do thank you; I thank you truly—for the foolish young fellow's sake. What claret this is, to be sure! Not equal to the port, you say? I have a bin of very good port myself, and if you will dine with me to-morrow, Sir Turtle, you shall taste it. Seven o'clock, sharp. Come a little before it. I shall be glad to see you."

Sir Turtle Kite, in his gratification, hardly knew whether he stood on his head or his heels. He had never, to his recollection, been bidden to an Earl's dinner-table before, and was profuse in thanks.

"I'll ask Grubb to join us," said Lord Acorn. "You know him?"

"Ay, we all know Grubb. What a charming young man he is! Young compared with you and me, my lord, especially

with me," added Sir Turtle. " So honourable, so good, and so prosperous ! "

Lord Acorn made quite an evening of it:
looking at the greenhouses, and the pinery,
and the growing melons, with all the rest of
the horticultural treasures at Rosemary Lodge,
and went back to town on the top of a West-
end omnibus.

CHAPTER XII.

INFATUATION.

MIDNIGHT. Pacing her chamber in her light dressing-robe, its open sleeves thrown back from her restless hands, as if for coolness, was the Lady Adela. Throughout the whole business she had never been so terrified as now, had never before realised her dangerous position in all its fulness. Her heart and her brow were alike beating with fever heat.

On the Monday evening, for we must go back a day, after receiving the news that her husband would probably not be home, as conveyed to her by note from Mr. Howard, Adela did not spend quite the solitary hours she had anticipated. Grace came to her: and though rather given to call Grace an "old lecturer," Adela was heartily glad to see her now. The evening's solitude had but intensified her fears, and dismal doubts chased each other through her mind.

Ever thoughtful and kind, though she did condemn Adela, Grace came to bring her the tidings that Charles Cleveland would be discharged on the morrow—for Lord Acorn, on his return from that afternoon's interview with Mr. Howard, in Leadenhall Street, had spoken of the release as an assured fact. The more bitter the condemnation by her father and mother of Adela, and it really was bitter, the greater need, thought Grace, that someone should stand by her : and here she was, with her cheering news. And the relief it brought no pen can express. Adela forgot her fears ; ay, and her repentance. She became her own light-headed self again, and provoked Grace by her saucy words. In the great revulsion of feeling she almost forgot her trouble ; nay, resented it.

"What a shame !—to frighten me as papa and mamma did this afternoon ! I thought old Howard would not be quite a bear ; and I knew my husband had all power in his hand —if he chose to exercise it."

"Any way, Adela, he has exercised it. You have a husband in a thousand. I do hope you will show your gratitude by behaving to him well in future."

"I dare say! I did think of—what *do* you suppose I thought of doing, Gracie? That if he proved obdurate, as papa hinted, I would win him over by saying, 'Let us kiss and be friends.'"

"If you could have so won him."

"If!" retorted Adela, a mocking smile on her pretty lips. "You think he yet cares for me a little, Gracie; but you do not know how much. I believe—now don't you start away at my irreverence!—that he loves me better than heaven. I shall not do it now."

"Do what?" asked Grace.

"Kiss and be friends. Neither the one nor the other. I shall abuse him instead; reproach him for having stood out so long about that poor wretched Charley: and I shall hold him at arm's length as before. The time is not come for me to be reconciled to *him*."

"You do not mean it, Adela! You cannot be so wicked."

"Not mean it! You will see. So will he. Tra-la-la-la! Oh, what a horrible nightmare it has been!—and what a mercy to awaken from it!"

She laid hold of her pretty gold-sprigged muslin dress with both hands; she had not changed it; and waltzed across the room and back again. Grace wondered whether she could be growing really heartless; she was not born so: but of course it must be a glad relief.

The old proverb, "when the devil was sick," no doubt so well known to the reader that it need not be quoted, is exemplified very often indeed in our everyday life. With the removal of the danger, Adela no longer remembered it had been there, only too willingly did she thrust it away from her. She passed a good night, and the next day was seen driving gaily in the Park and elsewhere with her friend the young Lady Cust—who was just as frivolous as herself.

Evening came: Tuesday evening, please

remember. Mr. Grubb did not come home; neither had Adela heard from him : she supposed him to be still at Blackheath, and sat down to dinner alone. She wondered whither Charley had betaken himself off on his release : and whether he would be likely to call upon her. She hoped not : her cheeks would take a tinge of shame at facing him. Suppose he were to come in that evening !

Charley did not come. But Frances Chenevix did. Frances, very downright, very outspoken, had been honestly indignant with Adela for the part she had played, she had not scrupled to tell her so, and they had quarrelled. Therefore Adela was not much pleased to see her. She found that Frances had been dining at home, and had ordered the carriage round here on her way back to Lady Sarah Hope's. It was about nine o'clock.

" Is your husband at home ?" she inquired of Adela, without any circumlocution, when she entered the drawing-room.

" No. He has not been home since yesterday morning. I expect he is at Blackheath with that wavering old mother of his, dying to-day and well to-morrow," listlessly added Adela.

" Had he been at home I should have sent him round to the mother and Grace ; they are so frightfully uneasy."

" The mother ? " repeated Adela. " Is she back already from the Dunfords' ? "

" She has not been to the Dunfords'," said Frances. " I suppose you know of the dreadful turn affairs have taken with Charles Cleveland ? "

Something like a drop of iced water seemed to trickle down Adela's back. " I know nothing—I have heard nothing," she gasped. " Is Charles not set at liberty ? "

"Good gracious, no!   And he is not going to be.   The city magistrates won't do it ; they will commit him for trial."

It was as if a whole pailful of cold water were pouring down now. " Oh, Frances, it cannot be true ! "

" It is too true.   Mr. Howard wrote this afternoon to tell papa that Charles was re- manded back to prison, and would be committed in the morning. Papa went off at once to see about it, and mamma sent an excuse to the Dunfords. I was to have dined quietly with Grace and Mary this evening; and I heard all this when I arrived."

"And—is papa not back yet?" again gasped Adela.

"No; and mamma can hardly contain herself for uneasiness. For, of course you see what this implies?"

Adela was not sure whether she saw it or not. She only gazed at her sister.

"It means that either Charles must suffer, or you, Adela, so far as can be gathered from present aspects. And the question at home is—can they allow him to suffer, even if he be willing, and the truth does not transpire in other ways?"

"To—suffer?" hesitated Adela.

"To stand his trial."

"Why does not Mr. Grubb stop all this?" angrily flashed Adela, in her sick tremor.

"Mr. Grubb would no doubt be only glad to do it—and Mr. Howard also would be now, but it is out of their hands. Once a magistrate turns adverse, it is all up. Charley's lawyer impressed upon the magistrate, one Sir Turtle Kite, that his client was not the individual who was guilty: very well, said Sir Turtle, bring forward the individual who was guilty, and he would release Charley; not before. Adela, we have not seen the mother cry often, but she sobbed to-night."

Suddenly, violently, almost as though she had caught the infection from the words, Adela burst into a storm of sobs. The revulsion from terror to ease had told upon her feelings the previous night, but not as that of ease to terror was telling this. What now of her boastful, saucy avowals to Grace?

Leaving her sister to digest the ill-starred news, Frances departed; she could not keep the carriage longer, as it was wanted by Lady Sarah. Adela sat up till past eleven, and then, shivering inwardly, went to her room, but she was too uneasy to go to bed. Dismissing her maid, she put on a dressing-gown— as was told at the beginning of the chapter —and so prepared to pass the wretched night. Now pacing the carpet in an agony, now gazing eagerly from the open window at every cab that rattled across the square, less happily it might bring her husband. She could see no refuge anywhere but in him.

The intelligent reader has of course discerned that it was on this same evening Lord Acorn was at Rosemary Lodge, making things right with Sir Turtle Kite. About eleven o'clock the Earl got home, bringing with him his glad tidings. Lady Acorn, relieved of her fears, took up her temper again, and was more wrathfully bitter against Adela than ever. But Adela knew nothing of all this.

With the morning, Wednesday, Sir Turtle Kite appeared on the magisterial bench, and the prisoner, Charles Cleveland, was brought before him. As before, the proceedings were heard in private. Mr. Grubb was present; had come up specially from Blackheath. He assured Sir Turtle that the prisoner was wholly innocent, had been made the unconscious dupe of another: upon which Sir Turtle, in a learned speech that even his own legal clerk could make neither head nor tail of, discharged the prisoner, and graciously informed him he left the court "without a stain upon his character."

Charles looked half-dazed amidst the sea of faces around him: he made his way to Mr. Grubb. "I thank you with my whole heart, sir," he whispered deprecatingly. "I shall never forget your kindness."

"Let it be a warning to you for all your future life," was the grave, kind answer.

The question flashed through Charley's mind—where was he to go? That he had forfeited his post at Grubb and Howard's, and his residence in Mr. Grubb's house, went without telling. At that moment Lord Acorn advanced from some dark region of the outer passage.

"You are going down to Netherleigh this afternoon with your father, Charles," said he. "But you can come home with me first and get some lunch. Wait a minute. I want to speak to Mr. Grubb."

Mr. Grubb appeared to have vanished. Lord Acorn could not see him anywhere. He wrote a line in pencil, asking him to dine with him that day at seven o'clock, sent it to

Leadenhall Street, and got into a cab with Charley.

"Oh," said the Countess of Acorn, when she saw the ex-prisoner arrive, "so you *are* here, young man! It is more than I expected."

"And more than I did—since yesterday," confessed he.

"Pray what name do you give to that devoted chivalry of yours, Charley?—the taking of another's sins upon your own shoulders?" whispered Frances Chenevix, who happened to be at her father's. In fact, Colonel Hope and Lady Sarah, outwardly anxious, and inwardly scandalised at the whole affair, beginning with Adela and ending with Charley, had despatched her to Chenevix House for any news there might be.

"I don't know," answered Charley. "Perhaps you might call it infatuation."

"That was just it," nodded Frances. "Don't you go and be an idiot again. *That* is my mother's best name for you."

Charles nodded assentingly. He saw the past in its true light now. He was a changed man. His confinement and reflections in prison, combined with the prospect of being condemned as a felon, from which he had then seen no chance of escape save by his own confession, which he had persistently resolved not to make, had added years to his experience in life. He was a light-hearted, light-headed boy when he entered Newgate; he came out of it older and graver than his years.

More severely than for aught else did he blame himself for having responded in ever so slight a degree to the ridiculous flirtation commenced by Lady Adela; and for having fallen into the worshipping of her almost as he might have worshipped an angel; and he thanked God in his heart, now, that he had never been betrayed into offering her a disrespectful look or word. She belonged to her husband; not to him; and to be disloyal to either of them Charley would have regarded as the most consummate folly or sin.

Was he cured of that infatuation? Ay, he was. The heartless conduct of Lady Adela, in leaving him to bear the brunt of the crime and the disgrace that came of it, without

giving heed or aid, had helped to cure him.
He had not wished that she should sacrifice
her good name to save his, though the whole
sin lay with her; but he did think she might
have offered him one little word of sympathy.
He lay languishing within the walls of that
awful prison for her sake, and she had never
conveyed to him, by note or message, so much
as the intimation, I am sorry for you.
Charles Cleveland could not know that Adela
had been afraid to do it; afraid lest the
smallest notice on her part should lead to the
betrayal of herself. What she would have
done, what they would all have done, had he
really been committed to take his trial, she
does not know to this day. However, to him
her silence had appeared to be heartless indifference; and that, combined with his own
danger and his prolonged reflection, had
served to change and cure him.

"I am very thankful, Charles," breathed
Grace, and the tears stood in her eyes as she
took his hand. "No one knows what trouble
this has been to me."

"I have more cause to be thankful than

you, Grace; and I think I am," he answered.
" It has been to me a life's lesson."

" Ay. You will not fall into mischief
again, Charley?" she said, almost entreat-
ingly. "You will not lose your wits for a
married woman, as you did for Adela?"

" If ever again I get trapped by any
woman, married or single, all courtly smiles
one day, when she wants to amuse herself
and serve her turn, and all careless neglect
the next, like a confounded weathercock, I'll
give you leave to transport me to a penal
settlement in earnest," was Charley's wrathful interruption, the sense of his wrongs
pressing upon him sorely. "But let me
thank *you*, Grace," he added, his tone changing to one of deep feeling, "for all your care
and concern for me."

Charles could not eat any lunch, though
the table was well spread. In spite of his
release from the great danger, he was altogether miserable. Lady Acorn talked at
him; Lady Frances, taking matters lightly
after her custom, joked and laughed, and
handed him all the sweets upon the table, one

dish after another. It was all one to Charley: and perhaps he felt that he merited Lady Acorn's reproaches more than he did the offered sweets. He had not yet seen his father and his step-mother. For the past two or three days they had been staying with their relative, the Earl of Cleveland; a confirmed invalid, who lived in seclusion a few miles out of London.

They all departed for Netherleigh in the course of the afternoon: the Rector, Lady Mary and the baby; Charles joining them at the railway station. What was to become of him in future? It was a question he seriously put to himself. Surely he had bought experience, if any young man ever had in this world; an experience that would leave behind it its lasting and bitter pain.

Seven o'clock—nay, some fifteen minutes before it—brought Sir Turtle Kite to the Earl of Acorn's. Sir Turtle enjoyed the visit and the dinner immensely—though he frankly avowed his opinion that his own port wine was the best. For once the Earl's wife made herself gracious; tart though she might be at times, she knew something of gratitude ; and Grace, who made the fourth at table, could not keep her heart's thankfulness out of her manner—for where should they all have been without Sir Turtle ?

But Mr. Grubb did not make his appearance.   Neither had Lord Acorn heard from him.

END OF VOL. II.

J. OGDEN AND CO., PRINTERS, 172, ST. JOHN STREET, E.C.

www.ingramcontent.com/pod-product-compliance
Lightning Source LLC
Chambersburg PA
CBHW060514030726
47498CB00004B/943